BUTCH BOTTOM
&
THE ABSENT DADDY
and Ten Other Leather Love Stories

First Edition

Published by The Nazca Plains Corporation
Las Vegas, Nevada
2009

ISBN: 978-1-935509-06-6

Published by

The Nazca Plains Corporation ®
4640 Paradise Rd, Suite 141
Las Vegas NV 89109-8000

PUBLISHER'S NOTE
Butch Bottom & the Absent Daddy is a work of fiction created wholly by *David May's* imagination. All characters are fictional and any resemblance to any persons living or deceased is purely by accident. No portion of this book reflects any real person or events.

Cover Photo, Fleshblack
Art Director, Blake Stephens

DEDICATION

For Gryphon Mac Thoy

*Lovers can find nothing to say to each other that has
not been said and unsaid a thousand times before.
Kisses were invented to translate such nothings into wounds.
-Lawrence Durrell*

*Even so quickly may one catch the plague…
-William Shakespeare*

ACKNOWLEDGEMENTS

Love Hurts first appeared in *Drummer* #162, April 1993.

Class Action first appeared in *Drummer* #179, September 1994.

Utah Connection first appeared in *Drummer* #126, March 1989.

Goddamn first appeared in *Mach* #21, September 1990.

Jacob first appeared in *Drummer* #211, August 1998.

To the Third Power first appeared in *Mach* #37, October 1997.

"Even so quickly…" first appeared in *International Leatherman* #18, April-May 1998.

Baying at the Moon first appeared in *Best of Gay Erotica 2003* and later in *Best of the Best of Gay Erotica 2*, both edited by Richard Labonté for Cleis Press.

Poz2Poz first appeared in *Just the Sex*, edited by Jesse Grant for Alyson Books.

Damaged first appeared in *Best Gay Erotica 2007*, edited by Richard Labonte , and later in an Italian translation as **Ferito** in *Best Erotica 2007 – Il meglio della narrative erotica dell'anno*.

Butch Bottom and the Absent Daddy first appeared as **Two Hearts** in the *Mammoth Book of New Gay Erotica*, edited by Lawrence Schimel for Robinson (London); and later in a Spanish translation as ***Dos corazones*** in *Tu Soñé Boca*.

A big thanks to all the great editors with whom I have had the pleasure to work. A special thank you to Richard Labonté, who has always been a fan and supporter of my work. And to the late Robert Davolt, *Drummer*'s last editor, whose encouragement was boundless at a time when it was sorely needed: Sir, you are missed.

AUTHOR'S NOTE

The stories in this volume are, for the most part, independent of each other. The exception being: *The Utah Connection, Jacob, "Even so quickly…", Baying at the Moon* and *Butch Bottom and the Absent Daddy* which, while not forming a continuing narrative, do include overlapping characters. I should not be surprised, however, if the characters from any one of these stories crossed paths with characters from any of the other stories here included. As in all my fiction, the names of streets, bars and sex clubs are (or were) real. The characters populating them, however, are completely fictitious and any resemblance to persons living or dead is completely coincidental.

BUTCH BOTTOM
&
THE ABSENT DADDY
and Ten Other Leather Love Stories

First Edition

David May

TABLE OF CONTENTS

LOVE HURTS

Sensual delight sickly and corruptively acquired
should be loved even more.

-Cavafy

"You're not too big to spank," Ken's father used to say. And at least once a week he did bend Ken over his knee, Ken's ass bare for his spanking. Where most teenagers would have run from their father, or at least challenged him, Ken went meekly to his punishment, handing his father the hard rubber paddle that had hung on the closet door for most of a decade.

"I hate him," he'd tell his friends. "I can hardly wait to get away."

What Ken failed to mention was the rubber he put on his hard dick when his father spanked him, a precaution he'd taken since the first time he'd cum while being spanked, leaving an embarrassing wet spot on his father's trousers. While he was certain he felt his father's dick harden and move beneath him as he lay bent across his father's lap, jeans and briefs pulled down just far enough to expose his butt cheeks but not far enough for his rubber sheathed dick to actually touch his father's

1

leg, he said nothing. To say anything would ruin the sweetness of the moment, deprive him of the moment his body shivered and his thick cock exploded into the sweet, tight confines of the Trojan. Each time he cried out loud as he came and his sweating body collapsed across his father's lap, his father would say, "That will teach you to sass your old Dad."

"Yes, sir," Ken would say sheepishly pulling up his briefs and jeans quickly to hide the condemning cum filled condom. "Thanks, Dad." And he ran into the bathroom to wash his face and dick, to flush the rubber down the toilet. It was a secret they both kept, their silence being their protection from the world's condemnation. But it was a dirty, dirty secret.

Ken's father died suddenly during Ken's first year of college. Ken was bereft, not only from the loss of the father he loved, but for the loss of the secret and someone with whom he could share it. To ease the pain of his father's loss, he went to a therapist and, among other things, talked about being spanked until he was eighteen years old, omiting the part about the rubber and cumming inside it as the paddle smashed against his bare ass.

"Do you think you may have actually liked being spanked?" asked the therapist, not unreasonably.

"Oh, no," protested Ken, terrified that his secret had been discovered. "I hated it!"

He never went back to that therapist again. Instead he found a man big enough to beat him up — and fell in love with him. But the man, a senior on the rowing team, had no interest in hurting Ken. He made love to Ken instead, drowning Ken in tenderness and thoughtful gestures that anyone else, Ken was sure, would have appreciated. When Ken suggested, and rather circumspectly, that their love making might get a but rougher, his boyfriend was aghast, called it sick and wanted to know where Ken had gotten such an idea. Not long after that Ken made a point of being caught with another man so his boyfriend would break up with him. Still, Ken was saddened since he had loved the rower very much. All he had wanted, he said to himself, was to share the secret.

Other men came and went during college. Some younger than himself, inexperienced and bumbling. Others were more sophisticated, unafraid to bite or occasionally slap Ken. But with no one did he share the secret, or show the paddle he'd brought from home. He caressed it only in secret, slapping himself with it when he was alone in his room. And while it felt good, it was never the same.

After graduating he moved to San Francisco. After his suburban hometown and rural college, he was hardly prepared for the intensity of the City, or for the discovery that other men shared his secret and discussed it with out shame.

Late one night while walking down Ringold alley, he saw man leaning in his garage doorway gently fondling his crotch through threadbare jeans. They made eye contact and Ken followed the stranger into the darkness of the garage. Before they could so much as kiss, though, Ken saw a paddle very much like the one his father had used, hanging on the wall. Even in the dimness of the garage, Ken recognized the outline of it easily. He took the paddle off its hook and handed it to the man, his eyes brimming over.

"Please," he said. "Please. I've been so bad."

"Sure, kid. Bend over."

As the paddle found it's mark in the darkness of the garage, as the sound of the paddle hitting flesh echoed out on to the street, Ken could be heard over and over saying, "Yes, Dad, yes, Dad, yes." And then he cried out loud, felt his cock explode as it had not done since the last time he'd seen his father alive.

"Thank you," he eventually managed to mumble as he picked himself up off the floor where he'd collapsed.

"Sure, kid. Now suck me off."

Ken stayed where he was on his knees and wordlessly obeyed. That night we went home happy, and slept well for the first time in years.

On Monday, as he sat with his sore butt in a gray flannel suit at work, his boss noticed a change for the better in Ken's attitude and performance. "Whatever is," said his boss. "Keep it up." Ken decided then and there to look for the man who had spanked him, to find others like himself. He was only following his boss's orders...

The next weekend he found the man again, standing in the same garage doorway.

"Hey, kid."

"Sir."

"I think you'd better come inside."

Ken followed, smiling, his heart beating faster in anticipation.

Seeing the man in the light for the first time, Ken saw how handsome he was, how the gray etched in his beard made him sexier than Ken had imagined. He also noticed the latex shirt that clung tightly to his body, showing the expanse of his chest, the ripples of his stomach, the thickness of his arms. The man pulled Ken to him and Ken sucked on the man's pierced nipple through the rubber, inhaling the sweet smell so much like that of the paddle his father had used (the one tied to his right back belt loop at that very moment), like the Trojans he wore when his father spanked him.

"That's a boy. Make Dad feel good or he'll beat your butt."

Ken pulled away a moment, looked into his new Dad's face, horror struck.

"Excuse me, son. Or I *won't* beat your butt."

Smiling, Ken sank to his knees and began working on Dad's cock until it was time for his spanking. Dad smiled as he put the Trojan on his dick and bent over Dad's lap.

"Wouldn't do to get Dad's pants dirty with your cum, would it, son?"

"No, Sir," agreed Ken, neglecting to mention that he enjoyed the snug feel of the rubber sheathing his cock, and even the smell of the Trojan when he opened the foil envelope. "I want you to spank me again and again, Sir. And, Dad?"

"Yes, son?"

"Could you please use this one?" said Ken handing him his father's rubber paddle. "I like it a lot, Sir."

"Sure, Son."

Ken laid across Dad's lap, felt Dad's big hard-on against his thigh, and took the punishment/reward Dad gave him until he screamed so loud they heard him on the street. He came into the rubber, filled the tight sheath with his cum, and collapsed over Dad's lap. Dad let Ken recuperate before sticking a finger into the tender bunghole.

"No one's ever fucked me before, Dad."

"Good, son. I think your Dad should be first. Don't you?"

"Yes, Sir."

A few minutes Dad was fucking Ken, ramming his cock into the well-spanked butt. Then it was Dad who screamed as he came, collapsing on top of Ken for several minutes.

"Here," said Dad when he gotten up, peeling off the latex shirt. "Clean this." He tossed the shirt to Ken and finished the order. "With your tongue."

Ken obeyed, dove deep into the dark, sweaty recesses of the shirt, lapping up Dad's funky, smelly sweat from the sweet, aromatic rubber. "Thanks, Dad."

"Do a good job on the shirt, son, and I'll let you do my pits."

Ken renewed tonguing the latex with renewed enthusiasm.

"Good, boy."

The next day, rubber put plug firmly in place, Ken went shopping. He found and bought a pair of rubber shorts that molded tightly to his skin, clearly outlining his cock and balls, and most important, his round, tight buns. But the rubber's tightness didn't help his soar ass cheeks. Every time he took a step he took he felt again and again the intensity of Dad's spanking. His cock got hard as he walked to work on Monday, the rubber shorts beneath his suit, and came as he sat down at his desk.

"You look chipper today, Ken," said his boss. "Glad you feel good on a Monday morning."

Ken smiled, nodded, and refrained from washing the cum from the rubber shorts until he got home. Then he jerked off with the rubber shorts covering his face. The mixture of latex and funk filled his nostrils. He shot all over himself.

"I don't know," said Dad a few days later. "I like seeing your bare ass when I spank you."

"Please, Dad. I want it so bad."

"Okay, son. For you."

Dad spanked Ken through the rubber, the rubber paddle slapping hard through the rubber shorts and making nasty, sticking sounds with each impact. With the sensation of being spanked coupled with the confines of the rubber, Ken came in minutes.

"But I'm not done spanking you," complained Dad. He pulled down the Ken's rubber shorts and finished the spanking on the bare ass. Dad didn't notice until he was done spanking and fucking Ken that Ken's cum had spilled from the rubber shorts and onto his trousers.

"Son," he said smiling, "I'll need to punish you for that."

"Yes, Dad," Ken smiled in return.

Dad found a cock and ball sheath made of black latex. Ken's fat dick got hard as soon as the latex touched it. Then Dad spanked Ken a second time until he came again, this time into the sheath.

"Now that got me hot again," said Dad. "I think you better give Dad some head, son."

Ken obeyed, swallowing Dad's beautiful cock as best he could. He choked when Dad's already huge head expanded and shot, filling his mouth with cum. Ken swallowed, grateful for the gift.

Sometimes Dad took Ken dancing. Dad would wear a tight latex tank top and Ken his rubber shorts. When they got home, Ken would lick the latex clean of Dad's sweat. This was his favorite job. He could never get enough Dad's funk on the sweet smell of the rubber.

The best part of all, however, was that Ken stopped keeping secrets. When he went to bars or parties with Dad, everyone knew that Ken wanted and needed to be spanked until he came. Everyone knew that he and Dad lived, danced, made love in latex. And while he was naturally discreet at work, neither did he tell deliberate and elaborate lies to disguise his life from his coworkers.

"You," said a coworker, "are in love. Why else would you be so happy?"

Ken only smiled and nodded, feeling his dick harden against his new rubber briefs.

"But I loved it when my father spanked me," he told his new therapist many months later. "He spanked me until I came into the rubber."

"Did you always 'come'?"

"Since I was sixteen. But I couldn't admit it to anyone. And we never talked about it. But Dad and I talk about it –"

"'Dad'? You mean you're boyfriend?"

"Whatever. I call him Dad. I never called my father anything but Father. Dad I feel close to. I love Dad. He loves me."

"And you didn't love your father?"

"Oh, I did love him. It's just that we could never be honest with each other, never even say we loved each other. And when he died, I —"

"Yes, Kenneth."

"I thought I'd have to keep being spanked a secret my whole life."

"And now?"

"Now I love Dad and I don't have anymore secrets. We wear latex everyday. I'm wearing it now underneath my jeans. It keeps my dick hard most of the day —"

"Yes. Well, I think we —"

"And best of all, my butt hurts all the time. That's how I know he loves me."

He left the therapist that day a new man. Now that the truth had been told, he never needed to go back again.

When he got home, Dad was there with an anniversary present for him. Ken opened the present and found a pair of latex shorts with the butt cut out.

"Dad!"

"Put them on, quick."

"Sure thing, Dad."

Without being told, Ken bent over Dad's knee to receive the longest, sweetest spanking he could remember. He came several times before Dad fucked him and let him lick Dad's sweaty rubber chaps and shirt clean. And because it was there anniversary, Dad also let Ken clean his armpits and crotch with his tongue, those deep recesses where the scent of the latex clung and mixed with Dad's own aroma.

Ken's ass was so soar the next morning that he knew that he would only need to think of how much he hurt to be reminded of how much he was loved. And as the years passed he often reflected on that particular morning with fondness. It was, after all, the first morning he was both free of the secret shame and fully certain of how much he and Dad loved each other. Then, with a satisfied sigh, he'd stretch out in his chair, feel the latex cling to him beneath his clothes, rubbing against an already hard dick, and think of what to make Dad for dinner.

CLASS ACTION

I kissed him that he might stamp me underfoot.

— *Frank Wedekind*

Todd, like most of his friends, slummed. He got drunk and had sex with men he wanted nothing to do with once he'd swallowed their cum or flushed the rubber down the toilet. But unlike his friends, Todd would talk about the joys of "delving into the loins of the unwashed masses." His stories about sex had cruel twists to them, barbed rejoinders that enraged his tricks (or "victims", as he called them), spurring them to new heights of sexual fury. That he left the men who fucked him wounded was of little concern to Todd. Unmovable himself, it never occurred to him that others could be moved, or even hurt, as he beckoned them closer with one hand and pushed them away with the other.

While Todd's friends fucked in the beds of men who lived by their sweat, had tattoos, or even wore dungarees to work, in the end they coupled with each other, set up house together and held elaborate dinner parties. Todd was disgusted by this incestuousness and announced that he had no use for romancing his own kind or for justifying his preference for working men. To his friends it had been sewing wild oats, but to

Todd it was a vocation. He needed these men and their untapped rage (rage he felt lurking beneath their amiable facades) and to match it with his own cruelty. Because he not only "liked a bit of rough" (as his friends called it), he liked to be mistreated by these men he cared so little for, and he did whatever was necessary to secure being the target of their anger.

"Where did you go to school?" Todd asked a construction worker, a man with massive callused hands that Todd hoped would soon smack him on the side of the head.

"Here in the City. Mission High."

"No, no. I meant college."

"You're a smart ass, you know that? Let me show what a smart ass is for."

And the man raped Todd's ass (after fucking his face and forcing Todd to choke on his own bile) in retaliation.

Sore and bleeding the next day, Todd smiled when he told his friends, "I knew I struck gold when I saw not one but *two* lava lamps in his living room." He and his friends cackled over Todd's coldness. Then they sipped their whisky and sodas, their gin and tonics, and went on to disparage, in tones just loud enough to be overheard, the out-of-towners with fizzy pink drinks at the end of the bar.

Todd held back from going to the leather bars because, as he confided to his psychiatrist, "I don't want a fantasy. I want them to fucking hurt me for real. What's the matter with that?" His analyst only grunted and asked Todd, once again, about his early childhood. But Todd knew that if he wanted to get hurt he'd have better luck at the bars South of Market. What he had not counted on when he got there (wearing dirty tennis shoes, jeans and a plain white T-shirt) was the over abundance of bottoms, all of them equally hungry for the same combination of love and abuse. Todd sneered inwardly at their neediness as he looked around for the genuine article, the man without affect. The bar was populated with obviously middle class men dressed as bikers. He knew their faces from downtown, knew them to be waiters, bankers, word processors, accountants. What Todd wanted was someone he would never see downtown outside of a construction site.

He let an hour pass, downing several beers while he waited. Finally, when he was about to leave his eyes skated over a pair of boots that looked real. These boots weren't shiny and clean like the rest of the boots in the bar; they were dirty, greasy, and well worn. The man wearing them was in torn blue jeans, a stained T-shirt and an equally worn leather jacket. His curly hair needed cutting and he had several days of a scruffy beard covering an adequately handsome face. Todd thought the stubble might be an affect, and looked closely at the man's hands for reassurance. The hands were rough, callous, the finger nails worn short from work and unable to hide the black grease ground beneath them.

Their eyes met a moment and Todd approached.

"Can I buy you a beer?"

The man looked him over a moment, then snarled.

"I don't think so."

Unused to rejection, Todd panicked. What man, especially one like this, wouldn't be flattered by his approach? Todd was tall, fair, good looking and went to the gym (the same gym as all his friends) three times a week. Who was this man who rejected him? Todd was certain there was some sort of misunderstanding.

"My name's Todd," he said, offering his hand.

"So?"

Todd was trembling now, his hand shaking in mid-air where he had hoped to make contact with this stranger's callused hand. He brought his hand back to his side.

"What do you want, mister?"

Todd met the man's eyes, swallowed hard and told the truth for the first time.

"Hurt me. Please."

"That's what I thought." He spat a wad into Todd's face, smiled as watched his spit dribble down Todd's cheek. "No. I don't think so."

He walked away. Todd watched him leave and knew with a certainty he'd never felt before, having felt very little of anything in his entire life, that he was in love. He followed the stranger out of the Lone

11

Star, watched him mount his bike and drive off with a roar. Todd caught his breath, ran for his car, and pursued.

It was not a long drive, and a few minutes later Todd was following him up the narrow stairs of the Night Gallery. Todd searched the maze of dimly lit rooms, finally finding him standing in a dark corner, one hand resting on his crotch, the other in a belt loop. Todd dropped to his knees and pressed his mouth against the thread bare denim, felt the cock move beneath the cloth, felt two strong hands grab the back of his head. Todd reached for the buttons with hands and felt a boot pressing against his balls.

"No one said you could taste my boner, blondie. No one said you could even touch me. But your a persistent little cocksucker. What are you willing to do for that dick?"

He grabbed a handful of hair and pulled Todd's head back. Todd didn't cry out, but breathed in, sharply, and looked up into the man's face, into the taunting eyes.

"Anything."

"Yeah, right."

His booted foot pressed hard on Todd's crotch. Todd inhaled sharply again. Then the man backed off a second, looking down on Todd as if considering something. He grabbed his crotch, his hard dick visible through the worn denim, as if daring Todd to follow, and left. Todd ran after him, catching-up with him outside. He was leaning against the wall, looking straight ahead at nothing.

"You want it bad, don't you, faggot?"

Todd nodded, his mouth too dry to speak. He heard footsteps coming down the street in the soft drizzle. The stranger looked down the street at the approaching people, smiled and said, "Kiss my boot."

Todd dropped to his knees and obeyed. When the people had passed, Todd felt himself being pulled by his hair again. When he looked up at the man, a gloved hand smacked him hard against his face four or five times. Todd's ears rang.

The man walked away again, this time turning down the alley. Todd followed again. In the back of the alley, Todd was forced to his knees, his face ground into the man's crotch.

"Now you can suck it."

A moment later Todd felt the thick dick harden between his lips, lengthen as it pushed its way down his throat. The man grabbed a handful of hair in each fist and fucked. Todd choked, swallowed, gagged but refused to resist. Tears filled his eyes. A mix of slobber and bile spilled over his chin as the man approached orgasm. He felt the dick head swell before it was pulled rudely from his mouth and cum splattered across his face. He licked the cum from around his mouth as best he could.

The booted foot once again pressed against his crotch.

"You've got a hard-on, you fucking pervert!"

Todd nodded. "Yeah."

Todd felt the sting of the stranger's hand across his face again. He groaned as he felt his own cock explode in his jeans, felt the wetness expand as it covered his crotch and soiled the sole of the boot still pressing against Todd's cock and balls.

"You call me *Sir*, you fucking faggot."

"Okay. Sir. I mean, yes, Sir."

"You got my boot dirty, you fucking pervert. Lick it clean."

Todd wordlessly obeyed.

"You know, you're not bad for a wussie sweater queen. We might make a man of you yet."

Todd lifted up his face from the boot and looked up at the man, his eyes brimming over with3 the same hope he'd seen in the eyes of the men at the bar, the hope he'd been so contemptuous of an hour ago.

"Damn, you pansies are all the same. Mess you up and you'll follow a guy anywhere," he said tucking his dick back into his jeans. "See you around, queer boy."

"Where? When?"

"What was that?"

"Sir!"

"What's your number?"

Todd told him, offering him one of his cards.

"You really are a little piece of yuppie scum, aren't you? With your little faggy trick cards, I bet you think you're just too smart for words?"

"No, I just —"

"Skip it, queen. I'll call you when I want you. *If* I want you. In the mean time, why don't you just stay there on your knees and wait for someone else who feels like fucking your pathetic, pretty boy face. But don't count on it."

Todd stayed where he was for hours, getting up and leaving only when the police came by and told him to move along.

Todd woke up the next afternoon with a raging hard on. He thought of the man who had abused him the night before as he stroked himself. He'd already forgotten that he'd fallen in love. Instead of thinking about the (still nameless) man he loved, he thought of other acts of violence of which he wanted to be the object. After shooting a wad across his flat stomach, Todd called his friends to tell them about the sexy stranger, to tell them about the bruise splashed across the side of his face where he'd been back-handed. He admired the bruise in the mirror for some time, relishing how shocked his friends would be.

Weeks later Todd was leaving his apartment and crossing the street to Buena Vista Park, when a motorcycle came to a loud stop. A familiar voice called his name. Todd approached the man with trepidation. Beneath the helmet, Todd recognized the eyes filled with scorn and amusement. Todd's dick was hard.

"If it isn't fuck-face, himself."

"How are you?"

"What was that, fuck-face?"

Todd swallowed hard.

"How are you, *Sir*?"

"Not bad. Horny. You live here, cocksucker?"

"Yes. I mean, yes, Sir."

"You're lucky day, faggot. I'm gonna give you some dick."

Wordlessly, Todd led the man inside.

"What's your name, Sir?" he asked in the elevator.

"Stu. But you call me 'Sir' like a good boy. It keeps my dick hard."

"Yes, Sir."

Stu grabbed a hand full of Todd's hair and, for the first time, kissed him, fucking Todd's face with his tongue. The elevator stopped, and Stu pushed Todd out into the hall ahead of him, holding on to his hair.

"You like being hurt, don't you, boy?" Stu demanded once they were in Todd's apartment and Stu had thrown Todd onto the floor by his hair.

"Yes, Sir!"

"Do you think I fucking care if you like it? I'm gonna mess you up, cocksucker. And fuck you at both ends. But I'm just here to get myself off – *not* to make you happy."

Todd cowered inwardly and Stu struck him hard across the face. Then Stu took off his belt and told Todd to stand up, drop his pants and grab his ankles. The belt whistled in the air as it struck Todd's ass, cut into the white flesh leaving it red and raw. Todd refused to react. He held steady, his muscles tensed against the assault. Sweat dripped down over his body. Then he felt the hard dick between his butt cheeks.

"I'm being a real nice guy Todday. I spat on it first. Next you'll just have to take it dry."

Stu fucked and Todd gritted his teeth. Tears filled his eyes and fell to the floor with the tiny pools of sweat that puddled around them. He heard Stu grunt, felt the heat of his raped ass spread through his whole body. He knew he'd cum without touching himself, knew that Stu's assault was what he needed.

Then he remembered that he was in love with Stu.

When Stu came, whipping Todd's ass with his belt as he fucked it, he screamed so loud that Todd was afraid his neighbors would call the police. Then he was pushed away, Stu's fat dick pulled out as roughly as it was inserted. Todd stumbled and fell to the floor.

"Come on, faggot, get up and get me a beer. Then you can get down here and suck my cock. I think I've got another load for you, maybe even two."

Later, after Stu had taken time out to beat Todd with his closed fists and fuck Todd's face, he relaxed over a second beer, half-smiling and half-sneering at his enamored companion. Todd, for his part, sat on the floor and admired his new lover from across the room. Todd's clothes had been torn off of him during the proceeding hour, his face and body covered with bruises. Teeth marks now covered his neck, and his ass was a mass of bloody welts.

"Hey, little fucker, come here."

Todd approached on his knees.

"Your pretty blond hair is messed up, pussy face."

Then he hit Todd again across the face and stood up.

"I've got to piss."

And, since his dick was still out of his pants, he pissed on Todd, pissed over his upturned, bruised face. Todd came with a cry, his cum mixing with Stu's urine as it covered Todd's precious hard wood floors.

"You're one sick pervert, dude. You get off on being pissed on in your own living room. One sick faggot." He smiled, amused at the sight of the disheveled, piss covered Todd. "Anyway, I've got to go now." He buttoned up his jeans.

Todd followed him to the door, and for the second time Stu kissed him. Then slapped him hard across the face for good measure.

"Had a good time, pansy pants? So did I. Maybe I'll call you."

"Thanks. Thank you, *Sir*."

"Yeah, right."

After an affectionate slap on the ass and he bounded down the stairs.

Todd searched for Stu for weeks, but was unclear as to where to look. He went back to the Lone Star, back to the Night Gallery, searched the alleys and scanned construction sites for a glimpse of Stu. He resented Stu the whole time he searched for him, resented the control Stu had over him, resented his own need. But he had no one confide this to except his psychiatrist.

"Being in love," Todd screamed to his empty apartment in frustration, "is fucked!"

A few weeks later Todd attended a summer solstice party, an annual orgy so expansive (spreading itself over three floors of a rambling Victorian) that it impressed even Todd's jaded sensibilities. Todd wandered through the maze of rooms doing his best to look unimpressed. Then he saw (as he half-knew he would) Stu standing in a dark corner

16

getting his dick sucked. Todd watched as Stu gently fucked the man's mouth, spoke soft encouragement to him, stroked his hair. Todd ached for Stu's touch. He trembled within as he watched, but did nothing. And then their eyes met and Stu smiled, Todd tried to walk by as if he hadn't been watching, as if he hadn't seen Stu with this other man.

"Get back here, faggot."

Caught looking, and feeling like a guilty child, he approached Stu meekly, unable to deny his need for him. Stu grabbed his face and kissed him. Keeping Todd in a lip lock, breathing hard, as he came in the other man's mouth. Finally releasing Todd from his kiss, Stu smacked him once across the face and smiled.

"You get upstairs and wait for me in the kitchen while I thank this man properly."

Todd obeyed with a nod, turning around only once to see Stu gently kissing the mouth he'd just fucked, stroking the strange man's dick. Feeling a confusion of anger and hurt well up within him, he hurried out of the basement and up the stairs. As he waited for Stu, he planned what to do, what to say. In his anger he thought of how he might pull Stu down as he had the other men who'd fucked him. But unlike those other men, Stu had given him nothing to hook onto, nothing to throw in his face to raise his ire. Stu had given him only the pain he wanted and was now willing to beg for, nothing else. But now Todd knew Stu was also capable of tenderness and he wanted that as well. He wanted all of Stu.

Stu walked into the kitchen and Todd sank to his knees, buried his face into Stu's familiar thread bare dungarees, inhaled the sweet-bitter smell of cum, sweat and grease. He felt Stu's hand gently stroke his hair, heard Stu gently ask him, "Does this boy want Daddy to take care of him tonight?" Todd nodded, looked up half-expecting the familiar slap across his face. Instead, Stu stuck his thumb in Todd's mouth. To Todd's own wonderment, he sucked on the thumb, Daddy's thumb, looked-up at Stu and saw not the amused scorn he was accustomed to, but a genuine smile.

"Yeah, I think this boy has learned his lesson."

"Yes, Sir. I learned my lesson, Sir." Surprised at his own words he added. "I'll be a good boy, Sir."

"And you need your Daddy tonight, don't you, boy? You want to make your Daddy happy."

"Yes, Sir." Then he swallowed hard and said the word: "Daddy."

Stu smiled and pulled him to his feet, kissed him, caressed him, slapped his ass.

"I think we need get back downstairs, baby, so Daddy can do it right."

They found a nook where they could lay down together. Stu gave Todd that mixture of love and abuse he'd seen others crave, that he wanted so much for himself now, the familiar slaps mixing with the less familiar kisses and caresses. Todd saw the pleasure in Stu's face, saw the kind of man he was. Seeking to please him, Todd buried his face in Stu's crotch, took the thick cock down his throat and sucked. He let the cock slide in and out of his mouth, used his tongue to caress the head as it passed his lips.

"Baby," Stu moaned.

A moment later Todd's face was buried in a pile a pillows while Stu's cock sawed in and out of his ass. Stu held Todd down one second, slapped his ass the next, then he laid on top of him murmuring, "Baby, baby, baby..." as he fucked Todd's ass faster and harder. Todd cried out as he came. Stu's fat dick pushed the cum out of his balls, forcing him to shoot, almost against his will, onto the mattress. Stu pounded into him again, screamed his orgasm seconds after Todd came.

Stu pulled out of him, showed him the cum filled rubber and laughed as he tied it into a knot. Then he laid down next to Todd, the sweat from their bodies letting them slide cleanly against each other. Todd licked the sweat from Stu's face. Stu kissed him.

"Yeah," said Stu gently. "This is one boy that needs his Daddy."

THE UTAH CONNECTION

Let my lusts be my ruin, then,
since all else is a fake and a mockery.

– Hart Crane

It started innocently enough.

My boyfriend, Craig, was working late a lot setting up a new mainframe or something at the bank – I won't pretend I half-understood it when he explained it to me. He had his own key to my apartment, though, and if he wasn't too tired when he got off work he'd stop by and maybe spend the night. But mostly I didn't see much of him during the week and got lonely. *And* horny.

Craig and I always had the same understanding about tricking: It's okay as long as it's safe and doesn't take away from what little time we had together. The days of crowded bath houses were a thing of the past, and cruising bars on week nights was always a drag, so when I wanted some action I turned to phone sex.

I had a little ritual for JO calls. First I'd phone Craig to say hello – and, yes, to check up on him – then I'd take off my clothes, lay back with a jar of lube and dial. All of which is what happened the night it started.

"Hello?"

The voice crackled with an electric echo. Long distance.

"Hey."

"Where are you calling from?" asked the voice.

"San Francisco. Where are you?"

I thought that he might be up at the Russian River or down in Santa Cruz or somewhere else not too far away.

"Utah."

"Do you always call long distance to jerk-off?"

"Yes, sir."

I heard my cue: "Sir."

"You a cocksucker?"

"Yes, *sir!*"

"Want to suck my fat dick, cocksucker?"

"Yes, *sir!*"

His voice had a new urgency.

"What are you wearing?"

"Nothin'."

"Nothing - *what?*"

"Nothing, *sir!*"

"You're a fuck-up, aren't you, cocksucker?"

"Yes, *sir!*"

"What are you good for, cocksucker?"

"Sucking cock, sir."

"Then get down on our knees and swing on my knob, boy. Get down and suck that eight-inch dick. Come on, and suck it, boy! *Suck it!*"

"Yes, sir. I'm sucking dick, sir. I'm sucking your big, fat eight-inch dick, sir."

"Feel it, boy? Feel that daddy dick ramming down your throat? *Feel it?*"

"Yes, sir! You're daddy dick is choking me, sir."

"Too fucking bad, cocksucker."

My fist was slamming up and down my dick. I was breathing hard now.

"Are you gonna cum, sir?"

"Yeah, boy! I'm cumming. Gonna cum in your mouth, give you my load. Gonna feed you my cum, boy. Gonna fill you up with – Ahhhh!"

I splattered all over myself, covering my flat stomach and hairy chest with jizz. My body relaxed. I felt great.

"You still there?"

"Yeah."

"You cum?"

"No."

"What's that?"

"No, *sir!*"

"I should slap that ass of yours."

"Yes, *sir!*"

His enthusiasm returned, doubled.

"Whip that ass good," I said. "Take off my belt and whip that ass bright red –."

"Yes, *sir!*"

"Whip it black and blue."

"Yes, *sir!*"

"I'm gonna whip that ass black and blue, whip your ass 'til it's bleeding. And then –."

"Yes, sir?"

"I'm gonna fuck it long and hard. Fuck it 'til you can taste my cum coming up your throat."

"Yes, *sir!*"

He was panting hard.

"Your dick hard, cocksucker?"

"Yes, *sir!*"

"You like getting your ass whipped and fucked?"

"Yes, *sir!*"

"Fucking pervert."

"Yes, s–. Oooh!"

I knew he'd cum.

"I didn't hear you."

"Yes, sir," he said meekly.

"You cum?"

"And how. Hey, what's your name?"

"Andy."

"I'm Chip."

"Hey, Chip."

Just like always, I thought: Introductions after sex.

"Can I call you some time, Andy? Direct, I mean."

"Sure, man." I gave him my number.

"All right," he said. "Talk to you later."

"Sure. Bye."

Shit, I thought after we'd hung up. What if he calls when Craig's here?

After a while I got hot again and started to jerk off a second time. My cock was rock hard and reaching up to heaven when Craig walked in. He saw my condition, took off his clothes without a word, slipped a rubber on my hard-on, and sat on it.

"Baby, you make me feel so good," he whispered as my dick filled his hole.

That started a wrestling match with my cock still inside him. When we were through, Craig's cum was mixed with sweat and drying into a crusty mess in the all hair covering our bodies. My cock finally went limp, the slimy cum-filled rubber clinging to my dick.

"I can't leave you alone anymore, Andy. That big dick of yours almost went to waste. If I hadn't walked in in the nick of time –."

I started to tickle him at that point. He tickled back and we laughed so hard we fell off the bed with a loud thud that woke up my downstairs neighbor.

By the next morning I'd pretty much forgotten about Chip – that is until he called back a week later.

"Sir? It's me, Chip. In Salt Lake?"

Omigod, I thought.

"Yeah?" I said doing my best to sound unimpressed.

"Yeah. I mean, yes, sir!"

The "sir" got me hard, and in a flash I was laying back with my jeans undone and reaching for a jar of lube.

"What do you look like, Chip?"

"I'm five-ten. A hundred, sixty pounds. I work out. I look okay."

"You hair, Chip, what color is it?"

"Brown. Brown eyes, too."

"Beard? Mustache? Are you hairy?"

"Got a mustache. Not real, hairy. You?"

"About your size except I'm dark. Receding hairline. *Very* hairy. Just shaved off my beard but I'll probably grow it back soon. Eight inches."

"Eight, sir? For real?"

"That's right, baby. Eight fat inches of man meat. Sound like something you want, Chip?"

"Yes, sir."

"How badly do you want it?"

"Real bad, sir. I really need your fat dick, sir. Please, sir."

"Beg for it."

"Yes, sir. I —."

"On your knees, cocksucker."

I heard him move his body. I had a sudden inspiration. My cock was already swelling in my hand, getting ready to explode.

"Please, sir. Please, can I suck your cock, sir? Please? Please let me suck it, sir. Then ram it up my asshole, sir. Please, sir. I need it so bad, sir."

I came right then, covering myself with spunk. I rubbed it over my flat, but very hairy, belly.

"No."

"Huh? Sir?"

His voice was so hurt, so confused, I was touched. Tough shit.

"I said 'no.' Not tonight. You want it real bad, Chip?"

"Yes, sir."

"Okay, cocksucker –."

"Thank you, sir!"

"Don't interrupt me, cocksucker!"

"Yes, sir. I'm sorry, sir."

"You want my cock that bad? You'll have to earn it."

"Sir?"

"Tonight you sleep on the floor."

"Yes, sir," he answered, his voice filled with bewilderment.

"You holding your dick?"

"Yes, sir."

"Let go of it. Don't touch it until tomorrow night, not even to pee. The call me and have a dildo ready. Got it?"

"Yes, sir."

He was breathing hard. I could tell he was turned on.

"Is it hard now?"

"Yes, sir."

"Think your balls will hurt?"

"Yes, sir."

"Good."

"Yes, sir."

"Understand your orders, boy?"

I heard him answer "Yes, sir" as I hung up the phone.

A few minutes later I got out my leathers and tried them on for the first time in months.

That was the only problem with Craig: He was still pure vanilla. He even came right out and said that seeing me in my leathers scared him. I was so in love with Craig, though, that I was willing to put my leather and toys away for a while, along with my kinky side. But now that I had connected with Chip, I felt something shift inside of me, the acknowledgment that I still needed some good old-fashioned kink in my sex life.

The leather felt good against my skin. Just the touch and smell of it got me hard. And I looked damn good in it, too. Damn good. My time at the gym had paid off. My chest and arms were bigger than before. My butt and stomach looked even more defined in my leather. But more than all that, leather made me feel so fucking hot that I knew I had to look hot too.

The next night I was putting on my leathers in preparation for Chip's call when the phone rang sooner than I'd expected. Damn, I wasn't ready.

"Sir?"

"Yeah," I snarled.

"It's your cocksucking slave, sir."

"Your balls hurt?"

"Yes, sir."

"Good! Call back in twenty minutes."

I hung up the phone and finished getting ready, not at all sure that he'd be calling me again. But he did.

"Yeah?"

"It's me again, sir."

"You slept on the floor, boy?"

"Yes, sir."

"Touch your dick?"

"No, sir."

"Balls hurting?"

"Yes, sir."

"You naked?"

"Yes, sir."

"Dildo ready?"

"Yes, sir."

"I'm in my leathers, fuckface. Smell my leathers?"

"Yes, sir!"

"Good boy. You want to lick my leather, don't you? You want to lick it so it's nice and shiny."

"Yes, sir!"

"Tough shit."

"Yes, sir," he sighed with disappointment.

"Got some grease?"

"Yeah. I mean, *yes, sir*!"

"Now grease up that dildo and stick it in your hole. Feels good, doesn't it, slave? Find that spot where it feels real good. Found it? Okay, keep punching it 'til you cum."

He grunted across the wire, moaned loud enough to convince me it was real.

"Touching your dick, fuck hole?"

"No, sir. Aaaah!"

"Keep it up, cocksucker. Think of my eight inches inside you. Think of how good it feels to have my bull-sized balls slapping against your butt cheeks. Feel it, boy? Feel it?"

Then I heard him cry out as his balls exploded out through his dick.

"Oh, sir."

"You cum?"

"Yes, sir. Thank you, sir."

"Fuckhead. Did I say you could cum?"

"Sir? I thought –."

"You're not supposed to think, fuck hole. You're supposed to do as your told."

"Yes, sir. I'm sorry, sir."

"Fuck that shit," I growled. "Suck me off."

"Yes, sir. I'm sucking your big, fat dick sir. It's still slimy from my fuck hole, sir. I feel it ramming down my throat, sir, choking me. Grab my ears and fuck my face, sir. Use my face for a fuck hole, sir!"

I shot my load, heard it splatter against the wall as it shot over my shoulder. No lie: I shot that far.

"Okay, cocksucker."

"Sir?"

"You were a bad boy, weren't you, cocksucker? You came without permission, didn't you?"

"Yes, sir."

"What's your address, boy?"

"Why do you need it, sir?"

"I'm punishing you, fucker. Don't call me again until I say you can. Then obey me to the letter."

"Yes, sir."

He gave me his address and I jotted it down, the pen threatening to slide out of my greasy grip.

I hung up, and as usual jerked-off again. This time I put on a pair of tit clamps and pulled on them as I came close to cumming. Then Craig walked in.

"You just can't be left alone, can you?" he said.

He stripped real fast, pulled a rubber over his hard meat, put a leg over each shoulder and fucked me. He shoved it in so hard I almost screamed, but bit down on my pillow instead. I was so close to cumming already that his fat cock pushing again and again against my prostate either felt so good, or hurt so good, that I came in less than a minute. Craig pulled hard on the tit clamps and I felt my cock and balls contracting as I shot my load all over both of us.

I just laid there a moment, spent, unable to do anything but tell Craig thank you.

But Craig still had a gleam in his eye. He pulled out of me, rolled me over onto my stomach and put his cock back inside me. Than he gave me another long hard fuck, the kind that leaves me limp under the best of conditions, sending me over the edge into euphoria. Long hard strokes pounded inside of me, harder and harder until he finally shot his load, filling the rubber as his body shuddered on top of me.

"What ever got you so hot and bothered," I said a few minutes later when we'd both caught our breaths, "is okay by me."

"It was the leather," he said. "I couldn't resist."

"Leather is okay with you now?"

"Yeah," he said thoughtfully. "I guess it is. I had a few fantasies about bondage and stuff, I just never thought it was okay. Until I met you, that is. And the sight of your hairy butt sticking out of those chaps was hotter than anything I'd seen in a long time."

I couldn't believe it, but my cock was getting hard a third time. I suggested he try on the chaps. He did and I told him to bend over so I could see just how cute his white butt looked in them. He wasn't fooled, but I still got to fill another condom with cum when I returned the favor of a good fuck.

I didn't write to Chip for a couple weeks, and by that time I'd lost interest in him. Craig didn't have to stay late at work as often and had more time for me again — just like he'd promised he would when the damn project started. Just as important, the sex, which had always been good, got wild. Craig let go of his inhibitions and out came the toys. He was wearing me out wanting to try new things all the time, not that I was complaining. In fact, I only wrote to Chip because I'd promised and I didn't want to be one of those "I'll call you soon" shitheads that never calls. I figured, one last JO call and I'd bring it all to a close, nice and neat and friendly.

So I wrote to Chip and I told him to call me on the Wednesday night after next when I knew Craig would be doing his volunteer work. I told Chip to be buck naked except for a dog collar when he called, on his knees, with a butt plug up his ass. As an after thought, I put in a snap shot of me taken at the Russian River the summer before. After I'd mailed the letter, I wondered if he had a butt plug or could even get one in Utah unless it came in the mail wrapped in a plain brown paper wrapper. I figured I'd find out soon enough.

On the Wednesday afternoon in question I got home and found something in the mail from Chip. Inside were two nude Polaroid's of Chip. He was very handsome, more than "okay," even in the grainy photos. In one picture, he faced the camera wearing only a dog collar, the leash in his mouth. Two huge puppy-brown eyes looked at me above the thick dog collar. A fat dick hung down between huge balls, above that his torso was a shield of solid muscle. On his right pectoral was a tattoo of a crouching black panther about to pounce. In the second photo he was bent over with his back to the camera showing the butt plug firmly in place between the lightly haired, muscular buns.

When he called a few hours later, I was in my leather, leaning back with a jar of lube and looking at the Polaroid's. I was already hard when the phone rang.

"Yeah?"

"Sir?"

"That you, pig boy?"

"Yes, sir."

"You're a doggy pig-boy aren't you?"

"Yes, sir."

"Is that what you want to be, another man's animal?"

"Yes, sir."

His voice had a new edge to it. It was hot but serious, not as playful. I thought of those soulful brown eyes in the photo, of the need I saw in them.

"I got your pictures today, boy. You're a good looking pig boy."

"Thank you, sir."

Then we did our phone scene. I told him what a worthless cocksucker he was while he groveled, licked my ass, kissed my boot, and shot his wad while I fucked him. Then he sucked my slimy cock while I pissed down his throat. Then I came.

You know, the usual stuff.

When we were done he didn't say anything at first, not even the usual 'thank you.'

"You there, Chip?"

"Yeah. I mean, yes, sir."

"You okay?"

"Sir?"

"Yes, pig boy?"

"Uh. I'm not in Utah, sir. I'm here in San Francisco at a motel on Harrison Street.

Oh shit.

"Yeah?" I said, probably too casually.

"Can I see you, sir?"

"Chip, I —."

"Please, sir."

"Chip, how long are you here for?"

"I'm not going back, Sir. I just need to find a place now. Can I see you, sir. I want to kiss your boots in person, sir."

I looked at the clock. Craig would be coming by soon. I looked at the pictures of Chip again. As turned on as I was by him, I knew I had to make a clean break. I hoped I hadn't made a big mistake letting it go as far as I had.

"I have a lover, Chip."

This bit of information didn't seem to faze him.

"Is he your slave, sir?"

I only paused a second before I answered him, surprising myself with the answer even though this is where things were clearly already heading between Craig and me.

"No, Chip. He's my master."

There was silence on the other end of the line a moment.

"Oh."

"He's going to be here soon, too, and I have to be ready for him."

"Yeah, sure."

"Maybe tomorrow night?" I suggested, knowing what the answer would now be.

"No, that's okay, Andy. I'll call you, though. All right?"

"Sure, Chip," I said knowing already that this was it.

"Bye."

I knew he'd never call back so I wasn't disappointed when he didn't. I just felt badly, as if I'd mislead him, inadvertently hurting him with my need to get off so often.

Craig did become my master, though. Not all at once, of course, but bit by bit. He learned to top by letting me top him. Then we switched back and forth. After a while we stopped switching altogether and Craig locked a collar around my neck and threw away the key.

We moved in together not long after my last conversation with Chip, and things just got better and better between us. I never told him about Chip, though, or why I was wearing leather that night. But we both found out who we really were because of that night, so I've always been grateful to Chip. Maybe it would have happened anyway, but I'll never know for sure, so Chip remains high on my list of good guys to this day.

I saw Chip in the flesh for the first time recently.

We were at the Eagle. Craig was standing around shooting the shit with some friends of his while he held my leash and I sat on the floor with my Calistoga. I looked across the bar and saw another shirtless slave sitting on the floor, also on a leash. He looked familiar so I nodded and he nodded back. I wondered who his master was, or how it was I knew him. I wanted to go over and ask, but of course I couldn't, being on a leash and all.

Then I recognized him. It was Chip.

He'd grown a beard and developed an even more impressive physique since those Polaroid photos a few years ago. He'd also added a pair of tit rings that accentuated the definition of his chest and abdomen. It was the crouching, black panther tattooed across his right pectoral, though, that gave him away. And those beautiful puppy-dog brown eyes of his. Those eyes weren't filled with longing anymore. The neediness in the Polaroid was gone and now they were happy, even peaceful. Probably like mine.

GODDAMN:

A SORDID SORT OF LOVE STORY

Each man has his own way of being betrayed.

– Proust

He wasn't the hottest man I'd ever fucked. There'd been hotter men than him before, and prettier boys. And it wasn't that he was even a boy, either, because he was about my age. But he looked up at me like a puppy dog from where he was kneeling on the floor, his big eyes pleading for something.

Dick? Cum? Love?

What could I do?

I beat him and he thanked me for it.

The whole time I was taking a belt to his ass – raising as many welts on the smooth hairless skin as I could because I wanted him to remember me for a long, long time – I kept thinking that he'd be even hotter in a slave collar. And I wanted that slave collar to be locked around his neck by me.

Goddamn. I was in love.

But let me go back to the beginning.

I was at the tubs and the only thing I was looking for was a little action. Maybe some head, maybe the chance to poke some hard, round butt. Maybe both. But that's all I was looking for. Honest. And then I saw him, this guy with the big puppy dog eyes. Good looking, but not that special, really: Around thirty, not what you'd call pretty, though maybe he was once, clean shaven, almost hairless. Not my usual type at all. But there was something about him. His eyes.

I loved the way he looked up at me for permission when he lifted the towel around my waist and put my dick in his mouth, the way he sucked on it and licked my balls, like he really wanted what I had. He wasn't acting like he was doing me a favor the way some cocksuckers do. I mean, he was really into it. And really into *me*.

I pulled him up off of his knees, wrapped my big arms around him like a wrestler, and kissed him long and hard. He melted. And he was so good. He did what I told him to do: Lick the sweat from my pits and balls, suck my dick some more, pull on my tits. It was so hot, so *right*, that I couldn't stand it.

So I slapped his ass.

"Yes, *sir*," he moaned.

That was enough. I took him back to my room and wailed on his ass good with my belt, like I said. When I was done, when my arm got tired, he crawled over to me and licked the sweat off of me. I liked that a lot. This guy appreciated the effort a man takes to beat an ass right.

"Oh, Daddy," he said. "Oh, sir. Thank you, sir."

Good boy.

I couldn't stand it anymore. My dick was rock hard and I had to cum soon. I told him to bend over. I was greased before he was ready. I grabbed him by the waist and dived in. I know I hurt him with my big dick shoved into him hard like that. He made some noise, but I slapped his ass cheeks with my belt a few times and he was okay.

Goddamn.

I filled up that rubber good.

I showed the rubber to him when I was done. There was a fucking week's worth of cum in that sucker. He was just so grateful that he got down on his knees and licked my slimy dick clean, then kissed the hand that beat him.

That's when I knew I was in love.

I kissed him some more and pulled him down on the cot with me. He fell asleep in my arms. I'd worn the poor guy out.

Goddamn I sure felt good right then.

It's not everyday that I fall in love. And I could tell that this guy liked me a lot. I just knew it. And my dick was getting hard again. I could hardly wait to fuck him some more.

After I fucked him a second time, I asked the guy his name. He looked kind of shy and said his name was Ricky, and asked of I'd beat his butt again some time. I said, "Sure, boy. Real soon." And I got his phone number. Then we spent more time kissing and licking the sweat off of each other. I was kissing his butt along the welts and bruises I'd left when I got an idea.

"You want me to beat you again some time?"

"Yes, sir."

"Prove it."

"Sir?"

"Leave your towel here and walk around the place so everyone can see how proud you are of Daddy's beating. I'm gonna follow you around so I can watch their faces when they see how beat up your butt is."

"Yes, sir!"

He jumped up to obey.

Goddamn right I was in love.

I called him a couple of days later.

"Ricky boy, this is your Daddy."

"Sir!"

He was so happy to hear my voice, I could hardly stand it. I wanted him real bad.

"You ready for Daddy?"

"Yes, sir!"

"Daddy will be right over."

I hurried over on my bike, just pausing long enough to be sure I had some safes in my jacket pocket.

Ricky jumped into my arms the second he opened the door and we locked lips like a pair of crazy teenagers. We were barely inside his apartment with the door closed when he was down on his knees and swinging on my joint. I got so hot seeing his nose buried in my bush I was about to cum gallons. Then the door opened and suddenly there's this guy standing there watching me get my head. Ricky was so into my knob he didn't even notice him at first, but when I got soft in his mouth and he looked up to see what was wrong and saw me looking at this other guy who just walked in like he owned the place.

"What is this shit?"

"Jon Jon!"

"You fucking slut!" yelled the guy, like Ricky was his wife or something. "I'm gonna –."

"You're gonna *what*, mister?" I growled. I mean, I was pissed. It was one thing for this guy to just walk in on me and my boy, but to start screaming garbage at Ricky like that... Well, I'd already had enough.

"You keep outta this," he said grabbing my little Ricky by his throat.

That was it as far as I was concerned.

"Fuck you, mister!" I yelled and bashed his teeth in with my fist.

The dude fell back on the floor, blood coming out of his mouth. Ricky ran over to him and for a second I thought he was going to fall all over the bastard and be pissed at me for protecting him. Instead he pulled a set of keys from the guy's pocket.

"Here they are! I knew it!" He got up and jumped back into my arms. "I went out with him a few times a couple months ago and he stole my extra set of keys when I –."

I shut him up with a kiss. I didn't want to know about his other boyfriends or why he broke up with them. All I wanted was for him to know it was okay between us.

The guy on the floor moaned.

"C'mon," I said. "Let's go to my place."

We rolled the asshole out into the hallway and left him there trying to find his way back up to his feet again.

Ricky practically lived with me after that, giving me that good head and tight butt any which way I wanted it. I slapped him around a couple of times a week for good measure, just to keep him in line. On weekends I took him out and showed him off in the bars, keeping him collared and on a short leash. A hot boy like Ricky you don't want to let wander off. And goddamn, I wanted everyone to know I was in love.

"What do you do?" one of the guys in the bar asked him once, acting kind of snide when he said it.

But Ricky didn't let it get to him. He just smiled big and proud and said, "I'm my Daddy's pussy-boy."

Goddamn! I could have fucked him right there and then. Instead I just put my arm around him and gave him a big kiss on the mouth.

"Daddy's *hot* pussy boy," I said.

Then went home and fucked ourselves crazy because we were in love, and when you're in love you can't get enough. I never got tired. When my dick went limp, I just spanked Ricky's butt until I was ready to fuck him some more. Or chewed his tits. Or laid back and told him to lick the sweat off of me. Or fisted him.

But it was never enough for me. I wanted to own him. Forever.

I told Ricky how I felt.

He just smiled and said, "But you do own me, Daddy. Body and soul."

"Good," I said and kissed him like I always did when he said the right thing, which was always.

But I was still afraid of losing him. I thought of that guy, Jon Jon, and how he seemed to think Ricky was *his* boy. Well maybe he was. Maybe Ricky got tired of Jon Jon and dumped him. And maybe Ricky would do that to me, and... I didn't like to think about it.

Suddenly I didn't like Ricky talking to his friends in the bars, or even on the phone when I could hear him in the next room. I didn't even like him going to work in the morning because I couldn't be sure he wasn't grabbing some dick during the day. And when I saw him smile at someone I didn't know in front of the Eagle, I slapped him hard across the face and sent him flying into the street.

He got up and glared at me. I felt like shit.

"Baby," I said. "What did I do? I'm so sorry, Ricky, I —."

He spat blood into my face, jumped into a cab and took off.

I sat down right there on the curb and cried.

I tried calling him for weeks after that, banging on the door of his apartment building until the manager called the cops. Even the cops wouldn't help me.

I thought he might go back to the baths because that's where we first met, but he was never there. I even tried sex with some other guys, but it wasn't the same. They didn't look at me the way he did. I knew no one else ever would. I needed my Ricky back in my arms again. Goddamn, I had it bad.

Months passed and I finally saw him again at the Powerhouse. He was with that Jon Jon guy. They were all wrapped up in each other's arms, kissing and slapping each other like me and Ricky used to do. I was so hurt, so angry, I wanted to break both their heads open. Instead, I just stood there and watched. Eventually they noticed me. Ricky walked up to me with a hard look on his face that broke my heart all over again.

"You blew it big time, Daddy. Now stay out of my life."

"But that guy –."

"You want to smash his face in again? Or maybe mine?"

"But, baby –."

"Go fuck yourself!"

Goddamn. He hurt me.

Now I wanted to hurt him.

I stopped going to work. Instead I parked my truck across the street from Ricky's apartment building on Laguna Street and watched the front door. I saw him come and go, sometimes with Jon Jon, sometimes with other guys – the fucking slut. Sometimes he was alone. But if he was alone he always saw me and ran inside before I could reach him. I always went home then in case he called the cops or something. I usually needed a shower by then anyway.

Guys would check me out while I sat in my truck, and sometimes they'd stop long enough to give me some head. But I always thought of Ricky when I shot my load, thought of what I wanted to do to Ricky so he'd hurt the way I hurt. It always got me off.

One time I was so into thinking about Ricky and how I wanted to hurt him but good, that I smacked the cocksucker's head real hard. He cried and tried to get away, but I grabbed his head and held it down until I was done fucking his mouth. When I was done, I pulled him up by his throat and watched his face turn white with fear. I thought of choking him since I couldn't choke Ricky. I looked into his eyes and saw the fear in them. Then I saw he was pulling on his hard dick.

I was in love again.

So I spat in his face and shoved him onto the floor of the cab. He just looked up at me and pulled on his dick. He was in love, too.

I drove to my place and I messed him up good. And he thanked me for it. He said he loved me, but I wanted to be sure he meant it, so I beat him up some more. He cried, but only in gratitude, and kissed my hand, licking the knuckles I'd bruised hitting him. I knew then that things were going to be all right.

Goddamn.

I didn't want to loose him like I lost Ricky, so I made him move in right away. I keep him naked and chained to the floor by his balls. So he's always there when I get home, and I never have to worry about him fucking around on me the way Ricky did. Everyday I ask him if he loves me, and he always says yes and begs to suck my cock or lick my boots. He keeps me happy.

I went back to work and said I'd been sick. They sort of believed me and I got my job back. I even forgave Ricky for being such a slut, and called him once to tell him, but he just hung up on me. Goddamn, I loved him, maybe more than I'd ever love this guy. But that's okay, because now I'm happy, and so is my new pussy boy, with his balls chained to the floor.

I never learned my new boy's name, or where he was from, or anything like that. And he never asks anything about me either. Maybe that's why our relationship works. We keep the mystery in it.

Goddamn.

JACOB

Loved is the man, loved his tomb
hiding his loving ways.

– Aeschylus

The flat I live in today, so modern and new that there is even a car park beneath it, stands where the Meijers' house had stood before the war. And the boys – excuse me, the young men – I watch play in their black leather night after night, are in the house I grew up in just across the Herengracht. Even without binoculars I can see them clearly enough at night to know what they're doing; but with binoculars I see them in more detail, enough to stir my ancient loins. Sometimes it's even exciting enough for me stroke myself until I climax, which is something to be grateful for in old man, I think.

The real irony, though, is that the games these young men play in their attic apartment were very real for Jacob and me during those frightening years of the war. And one of those young men, the American, looks so much like Jacob Meijer that when I see him on the street I can't help but stare. Sometimes it feels that I am as hopelessly in love with this dark haired stranger as I was with Jacob more than fifty years ago. And when this boy looks back at me, his face a question mark of concern, I turn my head for fear he'll see me weep, and then I walk away as quickly as my stiff legs will carry me.

Our home, one of the grand old canal houses for which Amsterdam is so famous, was also where my father had his office. Even today people are impressed with the house's pristine marble entry hall with its high ceilings – all designed to show off the fine but austere taste of the house's original owner. To the right, in what had once been the spacious front sitting room, my father ran his architecture firm. Down the hall was the rest of the house and its many rooms scattered over four floors. It was a spacious house for my parents, my younger brother and me. Even our maid, Jo, had a nice room next to the kitchen, large by Amsterdam standards, and luxurious to simple Jo who had come to us from the northern province of Friesland.

Jacob's family, the Meijers, lived across the canal from us. Their home was even grander than ours, and no office occupied the front sitting room where Jacob's family entertained guests, played music, and lit candles in the window to honor their Sabbaths and festivals.

Jacob was a few years older than me, so even though our parents were friendly we rarely saw each other outside the occasional passing in the streets. Even then, I'm sure he hardly acknowledged me, a shy and awkward child in awe of his exotic, dark features. It was only when he was studying architecture at University and began working in my father's office, and thus occasionally sharing our table at meals, that we began to be friends. I never ceased to be in wonder of his beauty. His black curly hair, high cheekbones, and sensual full lips filled me with something I didn't quite understand. I didn't understand it because I didn't yet know that a man could be in love with another man.

When the war came, when we were overrun by the Germans, things changed rapidly. First Jacob was kicked out of university because he was a Jew. Then the Germans starting rounding up the Jews, outraging the city we sometimes called *Mokkum*, a Hebrew word meaning "sacred place."

"No damn German will tell us what to do with our own damn Jews!" shouted my father at a passing Nazi, but not before my mother hurriedly pulled him inside and out of harm's way; men were shot for less during those years. Someone else wrote on the wall of the canal, where it would be hardest to wash off of course, "Dirty Germans keep your dirty hands off of our dirty Jews." We laughed at this knowing the insult would burn deep into the hearts of our hated "liberators."

I was terrified for the Meijers as well as others in our neighborhood, and scared for myself despite the German's propaganda of good intent toward us, their "Aryan brothers." Most of all I was frightened for Jacob. Somehow, though, Jacob escaped the Nazi's when he and his family were ordered to report to the authorities. He scrambled over walls and rooftops. Many a blind eye must have been turned as our neighbors saw his escape and silently prayed he'd find refuge somewhere – just not with them. Finally he found his way into our back garden.

Without a second thought, my parents hid him in the attic room filled with crates and odd pieces of furniture. Then my parents went into action. My younger brother was sent with Jo to her family in Friesland where food was less scarce and rationing a distant problem. Then my Aunt Dora, forced out of her home when a Nazi officer decided to take up residence there, moved in with us. This was the perfect excuse for me to move my bed into the attic while Aunt Dora slept in what had been my brother's bed. Now we had an answer should anyone ask why there were lights on in the attic, or why the attic was furnished. Best of all, though, now I had a reason to be near Jacob.

We slept in one bed. It was easier to explain than two beds should we ever come under suspicion. Behind the crates and old furniture that lined one wall was a hiding place, and beyond that a we kept a bundle of warm clothing beside a window just large enough for Jacob to make a hasty exit through it should the need arise. Though where he'd have gone from there, over the rooftops and beyond, I shuddered to consider.

Jacob was wiser in the ways of the world than I, and far less naive. I would later learn that he'd been loved by one of his professors, and before that by a boy in school. And only heaven knew by whom else. Still, my seduction was slow, consisting of long touches, lingering glances, the brush of his hard cock against my thigh through our nightshirts before my mother called us to breakfast each morning. Then, one night, as we lay talking about life, about the war, and what ever books we were reading, he leaned over, as if it were quite the usual thing, and kissed me goodnight. Then he rolled over and fell asleep. Or at least pretended to fall asleep while I lay awake wondering what the kiss meant.

The next day, I kissed him good morning, trying to be as matter of fact as he had been the night before. He smiled, ran a hand through my sleep-tousled hair, and roughly pulled me to him. Now his kiss had a very clear meaning. Our lips locked, our tongues fighting for dominance as he pulled at our nightshirts. His cock found its way between my thighs. I felt its heat, the drooling glands slicking my flesh as it glided in and out between my legs looking for my bunghole. I was too startled to struggle when he rolled me over and mounted me, not quite clear about what was taking place yet knowing there was only one thing he could be trying to do. His thick cock was so slick with it's own juices that he entered me easily. Too startled to resist, I gasped at the pain, and then the pleasure, that filled me as he fucked me, biting the pillow to keep from screaming when my balls exploded and covered the sheet beneath us. Then his whole body shuddered, collapsing on top of me, his panting breath echoing in my ear.

"I'm sorry," he said a moment later as I lay in his arms. "I didn't mean to finish so quickly."

I didn't understand what he meant, having nothing with which to compare our brief collision, and my face must have betrayed me.

"Don't tell me that was your first time?"

I nodded.

"Oh, my little virgin," he whispered. "I have so much to show you."

And I was eager to learn it all. What Jacob taught me, what I was eager to learn more than anything else, was to satisfy my beloved. I became the vessel for his release. He used my body as he taught me to be used by him. I never questioned that this might not be the usual way of desire between men because it suited my desire for him so exactly. As long as I was the object of his lust, as long as he taught me how to service and satisfy his beautiful, brown shaft, I was content to be used.

If he had beaten me I would have accepted it gladly at his hand. If we had met today, like those young neighbors of mine, he probably would have, and I'd have been grateful for it.

I spent as little time at university as possible after that. I studied at home instead of the library, spending all my free time with Jacob. Having always been shy and with so few friends before Jacob had become my lover, no one wondered at this. I had no friends to miss me at the coffee houses and bars that the other students haunted, no one to ask where I'd been hiding myself. My parents were happy that Jacob and I had become so close, that at last I'd taken an interest in something other than my books. My being at home also had the added advantage of disguising Jacob's presence in our home with my own.

Often I came home to find Jacob sitting in his chair reading, his cock already hard. Without a word I knelt at his feet, undid his trousers, and worshipped the beautiful, cut phallus before me. Wrapping my lips around my teeth as he'd taught me, I swallowed his cock whole, letting it slide down my throat as he let out a little groan. Putting a hand behind my head, he rocked back and forth, deep inside me, until finally, with a groan, his sweet elixir shot deep inside me. Pulling slowly out of my mouth, he let the still swollen head linger in my mouth a moment so I could taste the last few drops of manhood still leaking from the spongy, inflated gland. After a long kiss, I'd run down stairs and get our tea. Sitting at his feet, I served him first, eating only what was left when he was done, which was sometimes nothing but crumbs. Soon I learned what cakes and cookies were his favorites and began to ask for them, though the ingredients for such delicacies, indeed sugar and butter, became scarcer and scarcer as the war progressed.

I was fascinated with Jacob's hirsute body, its thick muscular torso, broad chest and high buttocks. I was so slender, so smooth compared to his magnificent hairy body that I never tired of worshipping his body, licking it, kissing it, as I sought to please him. He for his part, being beautiful and used to such admiration, took my adoration in stride as his due. We had no words for our relationship, other than perhaps "lovers." Words like "top" and "bottom", "master" and "slave," never occurred to us, though that is what we were. Having no other reference for physical love between men, I assumed this the natural form our love should take.

As bold as we were, we were never caught. My parents and aunt looked for reasons not to come upstairs and be reminded of the danger we were all in as long as Jacob was under our roof. For his part, Jacob only came downstairs when the office had closed and my parents gave the signal that all was clear. He used the toilet only then, as well, confining his needs to an old chamber pot during the day. I never failed to clean the pot for him two or three times a day. I not only emptied it, I washed it out with sweet smelling soap, and took pleasure in the lowliness of my task. My parents said nothing about this, either, as I was both quiet and discrete in my work. Jacob only nodded his acknowledgment when I had done this job, and that was all the thanks I required as long as I could be the vessel of his physical needs, the object he emptied his balls into two, three, four times a day. As frightened as I was of our discovery, I was never happier than when I was with him.

One warm summer night, Jacob woke me with his prodding cock, rolling me over on my stomach so he could take me as was his habit. The windows were open to let in the breeze, and we could hear every sound the night had to offer. I opened myself to him, let him have his way with me, feeling my own cock harden as his magnificent shaft filled my bunghole, knowing I would explode as I always did when he fucked me. He rocked back and forth, sliding easily in and out of me, grunting and groaning as he reached his climax. Then we heard it, the sound of marching feet. We both froze, our hearts in our mouths, as we listened to them come very close, then pass us by, finally fading away in the distance.

Jacob had stayed hard the hold time, holding me close. Then, when we knew it was safe again, he finished fucking me, holding himself back until I had had my own release. Then, after he came inside me, he pulled out and held me close. Rolling me over, he let me fall back to sleep with my head against his hairy chest. I noticed that the sky was already beginning to brighten though it was still very early. I fell asleep taking in the scent of his maleness, holding on to him for fear I would someday lose him.

Some other families hiding Jews were caught, discovered or betrayed, but we were lucky. Perhaps because there was only one Jew to hide in our big house, perhaps because we so rarely spoke about it even among ourselves, our secret stayed safe. Finally, just days before the Germans surrendered, we were liberated by the Americans and the Canadians, though I could never tell one from the other.

Jacob walked the streets again, felt the sun on his face for the first time in years. Old friends were happy to see him, startled to learn he'd been hiding with my family all through the war.

With the liberation, of course, came more problems. Jacob's family home had been commandeered by the Nazi's, and now housed the allies. We tried to make our new friends understand that this was Jacob's house by rights, but he was never allowed past the entry way. This pleased me, of course, for it meant we could continue to share the same bed. Eventually, though, when order was restored and the local bureaucracy reestablished, he returned to his home, now mostly empty of its original fine furnishings and fixtures. He waited there, supported by what could be found of his parents' assets and reparations from the government, for news of his family that never came.

I visited him everyday, letting him use my body as he wished. As the days passed, however, and no word came of his family, he lost interest in what I had to offer him. Or when he did use me, it was with an unfamiliar violence that left me shaken but no less in love with him.

"What do you want?" I begged. "I love you as I have loved you since the first night you fucked me. Take me again, use me, so I can feel loved again. Pleasure yourself and forget about me, but use me, please, my love."

He let me undo his pants and suck his cock, but never spoke, even when he spent himself down my throat. He only looked at me with disgust when he was done and slapped me hard across the face.

"Thank you, my love," I whispered.

A wan smile crossed his worried but still handsome face.

"When I'm myself," he whispered. "We'll be together then. Here with my family. You will be one of us just I was once a part of your family. You'll see. It will all be so safe and cozy..."

A few days later, when word finally came that his entire family had died in the camps, he hung himself from the ceiling of the once elegant sitting room. I found him the next day. My heart broke at that moment and never quite healed.

I never loved anyone as much as I did Jacob, though there would be other lovers over the years. None could make me feel owned as he had owned me. These new lovers sought to be my equal, when I wanted them only to objectify me as Jacob had. When I first noticed the handsome young men in black leather on Warmoesstraat, it frightened me a little – partly because they so reminded me of the Nazis, at least at first glance, and partly because I found them so exciting. Eventually I found my way to the Argos and its basement. For a brief time I found there what I'd been searching for, but after a while I was too old to expect a willing master, even in the darkness of the Argos' basement.

So now I just sit with my binoculars and watch those boys in the attic apartment across the canal playing their games in what had once been our private little world, our haven from the horrors of war, the room where Jacob made me his willing slave. There is a sweetness to those years, however frightening, that can never be lost to me because I was young then, young and very much in love with the man who was, for want of a better word, my master...

I was walking down the street yesterday when I saw my two young lovers on the street. One kissed the other good-bye, and as usual I couldn't help but stare at the American.

He saw me and nodded. "Good day, sir," he said respectfully in Dutch.

I motioned him closer and took out the only picture I have of Jacob, taken on the street just after the liberation. The American looked at the photo in silence, then at me.

"You loved him," he asked in earnest, but stilted Dutch.

"Yes," I said in my best English. "And he was a Jew. Like you?"

"Yes," said the young man, slowly. "Did he die during the war?"

"No. We hid him. There where you live," I said pointing to the canal house that had once been mine. "That was my parents' home during the war. He died later, after the war. He killed himself when his family didn't come home from the camps."

"I'm so sorry," said the American, taking my arm and leading me to a small cafe a few doors away. "Please come have coffee with me. I want to hear the whole story. Tell me everything."

He sat me down and ordered coffee for us. Instinctively, he must have known full well that I needed desperately to tell it to someone after all these years.

I nodded, yes, wiping away the tears that suddenly wouldn't stop coming. He handed me the black hankie that had been in his hip pocket and I wept into a moment, as he patiently waited for me to collect myself.

"Let me introduce myself first," he said when I'd at last taken my first sip of coffee. "My name is Jake." He extended his hand across the table in the first honest offer of friendship I'd experienced in years.

"Jacob?" I asked, startled, tears rushing again to my eyes.

"Yes," he smiled. "Jacob Meyer."

TO THE THIRD POWER

The chains of marriage are heavy and it takes two to carry them —
sometimes three.

— Oscar Wilde

The first time I saw Tony was near the back Loading Dock. I glanced up from watching the boy I'd just met cleaning my boots with his tongue. I wanted to be sure that someone was watching — because public humiliation isn't much fun unless it's public, right? That's when I saw Tony across the narrow room, saw him looking at us before nodding to his own boy to follow the example we were setting. I watched with a smile as Tony's boy dropped to all fours and went after his boots like they were ice cream.

This is cool, I thought, maybe we can do a scene together. Two Masters and two slaves sounded pretty fucking hot. I pulled on my boy's leash to tell him to stand up again. I wanted Tony, this hot new Italian looking man with his wavy black hair and beard that I had yet to meet, to get a look at my pretty muscle boy and see the kind of fun the four of us could be having. When I looked back up, though, Tony was heading out of the bar, his boy following him on the end of a leash.

Damn. Maybe next time, I thought trying to be philosophical about it. But I was still pissed so I smacked my boy across the face for good measure.

"Thank you, Sir," he said and kissed my hand.

A few months later I was bringing another boy home from the Power House by way of Dore Alley. The kid that was my usual type, muscled and pretty with a couple days stubble covering his chest and face. He had the usual tattoo on his right biceps, and pierced tits that loved to get pulled on. I was horny as hell, so I decided to take the edge off before taking him home to whip and fuck him. I pulled him into the shadows and pushed him to his knees. Without a word his mouth was all over my crotch, his tongue searching for snaps to the leather codpiece. Then my cock was out, glistening with precum and aching for a hot wet place to bury itself. The boy opened wide to take the whole fat eight inches down his throat, his lips expertly covering his teeth, his tongue reaching out to caress the underside of my manhood. I grabbed the back of his head and pushed him all the way down, fucking his throat with quick, sharp jabs. I was so hot to cum I knew that I'd shoot in a minute or two.

Suddenly, out of no where it seemed, Tony was standing next to me, his hand resting on my butt as it moved back and forth fucking the boy's mouth. I was only startled for a second before I turned to kiss him while I fucked the boy's face. His tongue explored the far reaches of my mouth, then let my tongue do the same to him. I fucked harder the longer we kissed, our drool covering each other's beards.

Tony broke the kiss long enough to say, "Good head?"

"Fucking fantastic. Want some?"

"Sure, man. Thought you'd never ask."

He undid his Levis and out popped this mammoth nine-incher, still hooded like some fucking cobra.

I pulled the boy off of my dick and told him to suck my buddy good or he'd get the shit beat out of him. Already primed from my cock, he managed to slide all the way down Tony's sausage with little difficulty.

"Pretty good," Tony murmured as he reached over with his mouth to kiss me again. "Pretty fucking good."

We switched back and forth, taking turns battering the back of the boy's throat with our dicks. As soon as one of us was close to cumming, he'd pull out and the other took his place, sucking face the whole time, slobbering all over each other.

I couldn't hold back my load any longer. I felt that hot wet throat wrap itself around my muscle and grabbed the back of his head and in a few quick fucks shot my considerable load down his throat. He choked getting it all down, but managed to do my load justice without spilling a drop. Tony's mouth was still locked to mine as the boy immediately went to his huge man meat, swallowing it whole. Tony's breath grew short and fast in no time. I held him tight as we kissed, as he shot down the boy's throat, feeding the sucker his second load of ball juice in as many minutes.

After the boy swallowed a second time, he went back and forth between or dicks, gently cleaning the heads and Tony's foreskin with his tongue.

"Fucking incredible," was all he had to say. "Thanks."

"My pleasure," I said kissing him again. "I like sharing my boys. Name's Hal."

"Tony."

"Good to meet you, Tony."

"Same here."

"Want to come to my place and help me work over the cocksucker?"

"I'd like to, pal, but I got my own boy waiting for me at the Power House"

"Hope my boy didn't suck you dry then."

"See you around," he said putting his still hard cock back into his Levis.

One final kiss and we were off in different directions.

When we got home, I beat the shit out of the boy, anyway, even if he did give my new buddy some great head. He enjoyed it, though, which only made my dick get hard again. This time I fucked his ass dry, making him cry, which also got me off. Then I let him cum before

I tied him up for the night and let him sleep on the floor, telling him to be ready for my morning hard-on as soon as I woke up.

A few weeks later I was on the prowl again, sort of looking for Tony, but telling myself that what I really wanted was a new boy. I scanned the Loading Dock for something pretty and sweet that I hadn't had yet, when this guy in a collar comes up to me, good-looking but not my usual type. He was blonde for one thing, and bearded, and as tall as me. And he was closer to my own age then most of the boys I picked up.

"Sir, my Master asks if you'd join him for a beer."

"Yeah?"

"Yes, Sir."

I scanned crowd and saw Tony across the bar watching us. He nodded and lifted two beers in one hand, and the slave's leash in the other.

"Hey, Hal, good to see you," he said when I'd joined him. "Glad you came over."

"Pleasure," I said watching the slave kneel at Tony's feet.

"My boy's name is Stevie. Thought maybe you'd like to come home with us tonight. We could share Stevie here and have ourselves a good time."

We chatted a while, taking our time to finish our beers as the Friday night crowd filled up the room. Then with a nod to me, Tony put his beer bottle down and snapped his fingers. The boy stood up at once and waited for Tony to snap the leash back on the collar.

"Shall we?"

"Lead the way, my man."

We got outside and climbed onto our bikes, Stevie behind Tony, and headed towards the Castro.

Tony lived in one of those little houses near Liberty Street, just a few rooms on a small plot built after the 1906 earthquake, the tiny garage an after thought crammed between the house and it's neighbor, and just big enough for our two bikes.

I pulled in beside Tony. Stevie scrambled off the bike and ran to the front door and unlocked it. We took our time dismounting, though, taking a moment for one of those fat, juicy man kisses Tony is so good at. When we got to the front door, Stevie was naked except his boots, jock and collar, standing at attention and holding the door open for us.

"Good boy," said Tony giving his slave a smack on the butt. "Now get us some beers."

Tony ran to obey and we made ourselves comfortable in the living room, crashing down on the couch as Tony put me in another lip lock. We were still sucking face when Stevie entered the room with our beers on a tray. He stood and watched until we were done, then offered me a beer before turning to his Master.

"Good boy, Stevie. You can sit down now."

"Thank you, Sir."

"You like him?" asked Tony.

"He's okay," I said eyeing him critically. He was well muscled but not a real body builder like the guys I usually picked up. And there were none of the requisite tattoos I was used to seeing on bottoms these days. His tits and dick were pierced, though, and waiting to be tugged on. But as I looked at him and his beautiful blonde beard – and not one of those sissy ass goatees, but a real full beard – I noticed how handsome he was. Not the pretty boy I usually went for, but handsome in a masculine way like Tony, only fair instead of dark.

"Okay?" Tony asked, obviously proud of his slave and disappointed by my initial assessment.

"Yeah, he's more than okay," I said trying to make a joke of it. "In fact, he appears pretty damn good from here. May I?"

"You're the guest."

I stood in front of the slave, snapped off the codpiece of my leather pants and let my hard dick pop out and slap him across the face.

"Suck."

Stevie opened his mouth and took my entire tool into his mouth with one swallow. I gasped as I watched it disappear. I put one hand behind his head and shoved my dick as far down his throat as I could, trying to make him gag. No chance of that, though, when he was used to Tony's even bigger poker. I just rocked back and forth on my heels a moment as I savored the feel of his hot wet mouth opening and closing over my shaft.

"Oh, shit," I grunted as I shot my first load of the night. I felt him swallow, gulping it down like it was sweet cream.

"Now what do you say?" asked Tony standing beside me and taking his own dick out for some suction.

"I say he's fucking fantastic. Let's party!"

"You got it, mister," said Tony shoving his cock down his boy's throat.

I grabbed Tony and kissed him while he fucked face. Less then a minute went by before his body shuddered and Stevie was swallowing his Master's load.

"Okay," he said putting his dick back into his Levis. "Let's put this boy to use. Come on, boy, show my buddy where we spend our playtime."

"Yes, Sir!"

Stevie led us out the back door to an old horse barn that must have been built when the lot was still surrounded by open country instead of houses. Inside the barn, though, everything was new. The inside walls were insulated and finished with the rafters left open overhead. The floors were refinished too, plane pine planks laid perpendicular over the original floor, sanded smooth and fitted neatly together.

"Very professional," I said with a low whistle admiring the inside of the old barn.

"Yeah, Stevie's pretty good at that stuff. Keeps him busy when I'm at work."

Tony ran his head over the slave's hair affectionately. I could see how much he loved Stevie, and how much Stevie loved him. I was jealous but tried to tell myself otherwise. After all, I lived alone because I wanted too. And I worked hard for the luxury of privacy. That's what I told myself, anyway.

"Try anything you'd like," said Tony with a note of pride in his voice. His hand swept out towards the wall covered with paddles, floggers, crops, and canes of every description. "We've got quite a collection."

I grabbed an English riding crop that had caught my eye and turned to Stevie who was already standing with his arms raised in the middle of the room, waiting to be shackled. I followed Tony's lead in securing the hanging restraints to the slave's wrists. Then I watched as Tony grabbed a pair of ankle restraints off the wall and secured them to his slave before fastening them to the bolts conveniently standing out from the wooden floor.

"Now," said Tony standing back to admire the bound Stevie. "Go for it."

I took my time working the crop across the slave's backside, moving across the shoulders, down the spine to the furry butt needing a fresh set of welts. Continuing the warm-up, I circled the stationary slave, letting the crop dance across his chest, dick, balls, and between his thighs. Little grunts escaped from the slave's throat, sighs and moans passing his lips, as I increased the intensity. His head rolled back as he cried out. Tears were streaming down his face.

I looked over at Tony, who nodded for me to continue. I put the crop aside and picked out a flogger, its numerous tails soft but heavy. I started on the back again, softly at first like before, letting the intensity increase of it's own accord as I circled his body with the flogger continually spinning and kissing the soft, pale skin. Red emerged, some turning bright purple with the promise of new welts.

"Yes, yes, yes..." murmured the slave. "Yes, Sir. Thank you, Sir."

I stopped long enough to kiss him, softly and tenderly, like I'd never kissed a slave before. Then I reached for a heavier flogger, this one's tails braided and each ending with a knot.

"Ready, slave?"

"Yes, Sir."

I started a third time, as softly as the whip would allow. His body writhed under its lashes, tears continuing to roll down his face. Then I saw that he was smiling through the tears, content. I let the lashes come harder now, driving him and myself over the edge. We were both covered in sweat. My cock, still sticking out from the missing codpiece, was harder than ever.

"How many more, boy? How many more do you want?"

"May I have twenty, Sir? Twenty hard lashes?"

"Yes, fucker, you may. Now count!"

I let the whip cut the air and into his flesh.

"One, Sir! Thank you, S–!"

The second stroke landed across his shoulders.

"Two, Sir! Thank y–!"

The third stroke, and so on.

When we were finished his body was trembling against the restraints but he kept thanking me. I stood behind him, spit on my hand and rubbed it over my cock, took aim and entered him while we were both still standing up. His head snapped back as he cried out from the assault. I continued to fuck him, ignoring his whimpers. I looked over at Tony leaning against the wall, arms crossed his chest, nodding with approval. I shot my load into Stevie's guts right then and there while I was looking at Tony, pulling out as roughly as I'd shoved it in. Tony took my place, not even bothering with spit, and fucked his slave hard and fast. When he was done he undid the restraints while I held Stevie up. When the slave collapsed into my arms, I lifted him up and carried him into the house, laying him down on the bed Tony led me to. Then I watched while Tony kissed him, caressed and praised him. Tony glanced up at me and nodded for me to sit next to him.

"What do you think of Stevie, now, Hal? Just okay?'

"He's way more than, okay, Tony. He's the best."

"I thought you'd think so. Come on, let's get us some beers. Stevie, you rest here until we send for you."

"Yes, Sir. Thank you, Sir. And thank you, *too*, Sir."

I spent the night with them, Stevie sleeping between us. Tony woke me up sometime in the wee hours fucking Stevie. He smiled at me when he saw my eyes open, and kept fucking. I rolled over and went back to sleep. When I woke up the next day, I had the usual huge morning hard-on. I got up to look for the others. When I walked into the living room to find the two of them reading the morning paper, Tony in his easy chair and Stevie on the floor, Tony looked up and saw my woody.

"Looks like someone needs a hole, boy."

"Yes, Sir."

The slave jumped to his feet immediately, reaching for my dick.

"Sir?"

"Bend over," I said.

The boy grabbed his ankles and I went to town, deciding to make this one a nice long, sweet fuck for both of us. When I finally came inside of him, I was sweating like a horse but feeling great.

"Good boy," I said smacking his ass as I pulled out.

"Now go get our breakfast, boy, while our guest takes his shower."

"Yes, Sir."

When I got out of the shower the house was filled with the smell of home cooking and the little sounds of a domestic life that I hadn't realized until that moment I missed.

Shit, I thought, I could get used to this.

After spending most of the weekend with them, I went home feeling elated, happier than I'd felt in years. When Stevie called Tuesday asking me join his Master for dinner on Thursday night, I was beside myself. It went on like that for a few weeks, spending part of every weekend with them and seeing them at least once during the week. It took me a while to understand why I was so happy with them because it had never happened to me before: I was in love. With both of them.

I learned a lot about them over those months. Tony and Steve hadn't started out as Master and slave. They'd met, fallen in love and bought the place they were living in before they found their proper places in the relationship. It had begun with a few hesitant confessions about sexual fantasies from both sides, then Steve gave Tony a paddle for his birthday and asked if he'd use it on him. They began role-playing at first, slipping into their roles more and more often, even when Steve wasn't wearing the collar Tony had gotten for him on his birthday. Then, when Steve lost his job, Tony figured he was making enough money for the two of them and made a proposition: If Stevie agreed to belong to Tony, body and soul, Tony would take care of him for the rest of his life. If

Stevie ever wanted his freedom back, Tony would buy Steve's portion of the house from him and set him free. Stevie thought about it a few days before agreeing. Then they drew up a contract, signed it, and Tony locked the collar around Steve's neck for good, putting the only key in a safe deposit box.

Each detail of the story got me hard when I heard it. I wanted so much to be a part of the story, even when Tony assured me that taking care of a slave wasn't always easy. "It's a heck of lot more responsibility than keeping a dog, that for sure," he'd say. All I could do was offer to help out whenever I could, which made them both smile.

When Tony had to travel on business a few weeks later and asked me to mind Stevie for him, I didn't have to be asked twice. When I drove Tony to the airport, he gave each of us a big kiss at the curb before running to catch his plane. Steve and I watched him disappear into the crowds behind the sliding glass doors, both us sorry to see him go.

"Tell me, slave," I asked as we drove back to the freeway. "Do we need to pick up anything before we head home?"

"No, Master Hal. Master Tony made sure we were well stocked with things you like to eat and drink. Is there anything special that I might have overlooked, Sir?"

"If I think of it, I'll tell you. So tell me, how often does Master Tony discipline you?"

"Sir, Master Tony hasn't found it necessary to discipline me in a very long time. The last time I was disciplined was because I neglected to keep my appointment with the doctor for my regular check up." He hung his head in shame at remembering this transgression. "I forgot that taking care of my person is also part of my duties. Fortunately, our doctor is also a Master and made me understand this."

I nodded.

"But Master Tony does beat me, Sir. Whenever you or he wishes, I am hear for your pleasure. Please use me, Sir, in whatever way pleases you."

"Have no fear of that, slave."

"Yes, Sir! Thank you Sir!"

We got back to the house and I told Steve to go wait for me inside the shed. He ran to obey while I stopped to think about the best way to find out what was going on between my new pal, his slave, and me.

When I stepped into the barn, Steve was standing naked in the middle of the room waiting at attention. I walked around him once or twice before barking my first order.

"Sawhorse!"

"Yes, Sir!"

He pulled the padded sawhorse from its corner and bent over it, his legs spread wide and his arms reaching over the other side to the floor. I pulled a nice thin cane from the wall. I swished it through the air a few times as a warning before swatting his furry ass with it, raising an immediate welt, much to my satisfaction.

"Master Tony loves you, isn't that right, boy?"

A swat.

"Yes, Sir!"

"And you love Master Tony?"

"Yes, Sir!"

Another swat.

He flinched this time, but kept steady. Sweat was already covering much of his body. Two welts were rising across his buttocks now. My dick was already hard, dripping and ready inside by jeans.

"You know why I'm caning you, boy?"

"Because it pleases you, Sir?"

Swat!

Another flinch. And a little blood this time.

"Yes, it pleases me to cane you. But why *should* it please me to cane you? Caning is a lot of work isn't it?"

"Yes, Sir, it is work to keep a slave in line. Are you punishing me, Sir?"

Swat!

A tiny cry was squelched deep inside his throat this time. I heard just the beginning of it, but recognized it for what it was: Fear.

"I am not punishing you. You have not displeased me in any way. Yet."

"Yes, Sir. Thank you, Sir."

"Now tell me, slave. Why do you think I'm caning you? Think carefully, slave. I will reward you if you have the courage to answer me correctly."

There was a pause. Even without looking at his face I knew that he knew the answer. He was summing up the courage to say it, the courage to face the consequences if he was wrong.

"I'm waiting, slave. Answer me or I *will* punish you!"

"Sir, do you beat me because you *love* me?"

This time I let go with everything, drawing more blood than before, bringing a cry from his lips before he could stifle it.

Swat!

"That's right, slave, because I *love* you."

I pulled him to his feet and held him tight, kissed him hard, holding him tighter as my kiss was returned.

"Thank you, Sir," me managed to say with a trembling voice. "Thank you for hurting me so I'd know you love me, Sir."

"Good boy," I said rubbing the welts on his hairy ass. "Now tell me honestly, do you love me?"

"Yes, Sir, I love you."

"Can you serve two Masters, boy, if Master Tony says too?"

"Yes, Sir! And I want to serve you both, too, Sir. If you are willing to be my Master, too, to share me with Master Tony, Sir."

"But will he share you with me?"

"He asked me a few weeks ago if I wanted two Masters, Sir."

"And?"

A pause as he licked his lips.

"I told him, yes, if one of them was you, Sir. But that it was for him to decide."

"Of course," I said fingering his butt hole. "I have only one more question to ask then, and that will have to wait for Master Tony."

"Yes, Sir. But I believe the answer will be worth waiting for, Sir."

"Good boy. Now bend over the sawhorse again and spread your cheeks."

He obeyed instantly. I pulled my now raging hard-on out of my Levis and aimed at the sweet little fuck hole I'd come to know so well.

With a little spit and one push I was all the way inside him, feeling the tight, smooth walls of his fuck hole squeeze my fat cock for all they were worth.

"Since you were brave enough to answer my question, Stevie, I'm going to give you you're reward now."

"Thank you, Sir."

"You may touch yourself while I fuck you, boy, and you may cum – *when* I cum."

"Yes, Sir, Master Hal! Thank you, Sir!"

I fucked him long and hard, giving him as much pleasure as I could, holding back for as long as I could. We were both covered with sweat when I reached the point of no return. I was pounding deep inside of him, my balls slapping against his butt with every shove.

"Now!" I screamed. "Cum now, fuckhole! Now!"

I shot my load deep inside him. I felt his asshole spasm around my cock as he came, milking more cum from my balls. I collapsed on top of him. The funky, sweet smell of man sex filled the air. Still panting, I stood up and pulled out of him.

"Now clean this mess up, boy. Then you can come inside and polish my leathers."

"Yes, Sir. Thank you, Sir. May I kiss your boots now, Sir? To show my gratitude?"

"Later, cocksucker. You can show your gratitude later."

"Yes, Sir. Thank you, Sir."

I took him out that night on his leash, let him lick my boots in the Loading Dock, fucked his face in one of the nearby alleys, and generally showed him a good time. First thing the next morning, as I did every morning I spent with him, I fucked him with my morning woody. The week passed quickly. When Tony got home, I met him at the airport alone, giving him a great big kiss the moment I saw him.

"Where's the boy?"

"At home making you a special home coming dinner."

"He's something else, isn't he?"

"Yeah, he's pretty special. And so are you, Tony."

"You think so, buddy?"

"I know so. You know what else I know? I know I love you and Stevie."

Tony just looked at me, perhaps a little amazed.

"And I think you and Stevie love me, too, Tony."

"You know what I think, Hal?"

"What?"

"I think you're right. You're family now, buddy. I think it's time to make this official."

On Stevie's next birthday, after his flogging and after we'd fucked him and let him cum, we brought him inside and let him open his presents. Besides the usual new shackles, paddles and floggers, we gave him a few books and a pair leather shorts with a zipper up the butt. Stevie was delighted with all his presents, overwhelmed at the number of presents.

Then Tony pulled out the slave contract and showed it Stevie.

"You know what this is, slave?"

"Yes, Sir. It's the slave contract, Sir."

"That's right, boy, it is. I think it's time we made a change in it, though."

"Yes, Sir?"

With that, Tony put a match to it and we watched Stevie as he looked on in wide-eyed horror. Then Stevie bowed his head, waiting.

"Open this!"

Tony handed him the last small package, flat in an envelope but wrapped in birthday paper. Stevie opened the birthday present. Inside was a new slave contract, just like the old one but with my name added beside Tony's.

Stevie's eyes welled up with tears as he dropped to the floor to kiss our boots in gratitude.

"Get up, cocksucker!" I barked. "No one's signed anything yet."

"Yes, Sir. May I please sign it, Sir?"

I handed him a pen and he signed it with a trembling hand. Then Tony signed it. Then I did.

"Well, that's that," I said. "Your ass is ours now, boy."

"Yes, Sir. Thank you, Sir."

"So Master Tony and I have decided to take you out to dinner tonight to celebrate."

"Thank you, Sir!"

"But the moment we get home, boy..." added Tony.

"Sir?"

"We're going to make you earn it."

While Stevie was getting dressed to go out, I held Tony close and gave him a big kiss. "Thanks, buddy," I said. "Thanks for everything."

Tony smiled.

"Don't thank me yet. You don't know what you're in for."

"I think I know all right," I said. "And I think I'm going to like it fine."

When Stevie came back into the living room we were still kissing. We pulled him towards us and let him join in the kiss. After all, we had a lot to celebrate tonight. Time enough for discipline tomorrow.

"EVEN SO QUICKLY..."

Love is like a fever that comes and goes
quite independently of the will.

– Stendhal

It had been too long.

It was not that Jon had led a monk's life since Ben's death. He'd fucked and been fucked, spanked and been spanked, often enough over the past two years to retain something of a reputation, even in a city as jaded as Los Angeles. But to give himself to another man, as he had given himself to Ben – to love and be loved, to own and be owned – had been impossible, not even worth considering. He had assumed until this moment that he was no longer capable of such devotion, of such submission to another man's hand.

But now Jon stood in front of the open door that revealed a burly, broad shouldered man, a large mustache crossing a handsome Nordic face. The stranger sat on the cot wearing black leather boots and gloves, and a deliberately too small jockstrap, threadbare and straining to conceal its contents.

Yes, the man is something of an archetype, Jon thought, but there is a lot to be said for archetypes, for the overt sexuality we used to take for granted.

Jon had not expected to find it here at the baths sitting on a cot and staring him down with the kind of sexual bravado that Ben had had. It was the kind of assurance rooted in the certain knowledge that he possessed exactly what Jon wanted and needed: Power and strength.

Jon paused only long enough to be certain that the man wanted him. He entered with bowed head, let the towel wrapped around his waist drop to the floor, and knelt before the man. Without a word, he reached out his tongue and licked the man's boots, nuzzling the black leather, the sweet smell of it mixing with the man's own scent. When he heard the stranger's voice, felt the rough hand on the back of his head, his heart beat wildly inside him.

"Know your place, don't you, boy?"

"Yes, sir."

"And you know that I've got what you want?"

"Yes, sir."

"And you're ready to serve me, to be mine for as long as I want you?"

"Yes, sir."

"Then I think we're ready to start. Present yourself!"

Jon obeyed automatically, scrambling to his feet. A gloved hand ran over his chest, his back, face and butt cheeks. A slap landed loudly on each ass cheek and Jon felt his dick reach upward in response. The man smiled.

"Good boy."

Taking Jon's face in both of his hands, the stranger kissed him long and hard.

Then it began, an adventure that lasted hours. Jon licked the man's boots again, soaked the smelly jockstrap in his own saliva, was spanked over the stranger's knee, then tied-up and teased with hot wax. Jon obeyed instantly through out, begging for more – more dick, more pain, more kisses.

The kisses were bestowed freely at first, then withheld until Jon's cries of pleasure turned to pain, until tears were in his eyes as he begged to taste the stranger's mouth again. Then, when he'd been fucked and allowed to cum himself, laying in a pool of cum, sweat and hardened wax, the stranger held him close and kissed him again. He kissed Jon longingly, sweetly and Jon felt their bodies slide against each other. Each kiss that fed him even as it increased his longing for more, like sea water that could never quench his thirst.

"Got a name?"

"Jon."

"I'm Craig."

Since it was late when they finished, Craig gave John a ride over the bridge and back into the City.

"L.A., huh?" asked Craig.

"Afraid so."

"Too bad."

"Glad you think so. But I'll be here a week, until the day after the parade. Maybe we could –."

"Maybe. But I have a lover."

"Oh."

"He's out of town right now, though. So we can probably get together again during the week. He's not into leather anymore, so..."

"Too bad. A three way would be hot."

Craig laughed.

"What about you? Boyfriend?"

Jon paused before answering, never quite sure of what to say.

"Widowed."

"Oh, I'm sorry. Happens more and more, doesn't it?"

"Too often. But it's been a couple years and I do okay. I just never... Until tonight I never let myself go like that, not since Ben died."

"Can I ask how long you were together, or would you rather...?"

"No, I don't mind. I kind of like talking about him. Keeps me from forgetting what we had. Anyway, we were together almost nine years before he died."

"We've only been together five."

"Good for you."

There was a pause in the conversation.

"Did you say I was the first since...?"

"The first time I let myself go like that. I mean, I never stopped fucking. I just haven't let anyone do what you did tonight, take control like that."

"You mean, Master you?"

"Yeah."

"I'm flattered. I was glad when you came in because I'd spotted you before. You're a hot man, Jon."

"Thanks."

"When you got down and licked my boots, I thought, Whoever he is, I sure like his style. But one question."

"Yeah?"

"Why me?"

"I don't know. The look in your eyes, something I understood."

They drove over the bridge in silence for a while.

"Did I scare you?" asked Jon. "I really don't expect more from you then a good time. I mean, I understand –."

"No. Well, yes. Maybe a little. Or maybe I scare myself."

Jon smiled to himself.

"But I want to see you again, get even raunchier with you."

"Great."

"Like to be flogged?"

"Yes, sir!"

"Damn. You're my kind of guy, Jon. Now I'm hard again."

"Too bad."

"Maybe not."

A few minutes later they were parked in alley south of Market Street, Craig fucking Jon in the back seat. Craig's fat cock, encased in rubber, pounded into Jon's butt from behind, again and again. His sweat poured off of him and across Jon's back.

"Like it, fuck hole? Like it?"

"Yes, sir. Yes, sir. Yes, sir...."

Then Craig collapsed on top of Jon, shuddered, gave a loud grunt and filled the condom with even more cum than the one before.

"Oh, yeah," said Jon. "Oh, yeah."

After driving Jon to his friend's house on 16th Street, there was a long kiss in the car before Jon got out.

"I'll be calling you."

"Thanks."

After the exchange of several calls left on answering machines, the two met for coffee at the Cafe Flore. They chatted like two kids falling in love, astounded at how much they had in common. When they parted, there was a long kiss on the sidewalk.

"See you Friday at the party, then?"

"I'll be there on time and ready to serve."

"Jonny, you're getting me hard."

Jon flushed with pleasure at the endearment but kept his cool.

"Too bad." A pause. "Sir."

"I'll remember that."

"Yes, sir."

Another kiss and a slap on the butt.

Jon couldn't remember the last time he felt so alive. His whole body tingled, revitalized.

"If nothing else," he told his friend, Jake, a few minutes later. "I know I'm not dead inside like I thought I was. When Ben died I never expected.... Anyway, now I know I can care about another guy again. I'll go home a new man. I owe him a lot."

Jake laughed. "And I'm sure you'll do your best to repay him."

"Damn straight."

When Jon found Craig at the dungeon party a few nights later, he fell immediately to his knees and nuzzled the man's crotch affectionately, sucking obediently on the gloved finger offered him. Eventually Jon was led into the dungeon and strung between two rafters. The flogging began, the gentle thud of soft leather against his broad back and round ass, and tears came to Jon's eyes, tears of pleasure and gratitude.

Why, he wondered for the first time in years. Why do I love this so? Why does a whip in the right hand feed my heart as nothing else can? And the answer came to him as it had come to him years before: What the fuck does it matter?

The whip was passed to other men, friends of Craig, who took turns adding to the now red, now purple marks that covered Jon's body. Craig held and kissed him throughout. He caressed Jon's face, cleaned off the sweet, silent tears of joy with kisses, held the trembling body when it was over. Both were hard. A few minutes later they were fucking.

They exchanged addresses before they parted, agreed to meet again when Craig's work took him to Los Angeles. Or Jon could easily come for a long weekend when Craig's lover was out of town. Somehow, they decided, they would be together again, and when they did, they were both reasonably certain, the fire between them would still be burning.

Their letters were regular. At first Craig wrote describing his plans for Jon, the new levels of pain and subservience he wanted to take Jon to soon. Jon wrote all his letters to "Sir," offering himself again and again to Craig. As time passed, the letters included more and more of their lives and less and less of the sexual fantasy. The only constant was that Craig addressed his letters to "boy" and signed them "Your Master," while Jon addressed his to "Sir," and signed them "Obediently." Both read the early letters over and over while jerking off, Craig hiding his from the man who shared his life because it was so obvious from them that he and Jon were in love.

Craig's plans for business travel to Los Angeles were canceled. Jon, too busy and too popular (now that he'd emerged from the seclusion of his years of mourning) never made definite plans to return to San Francisco. If pressed, Jon would have admitted that his reluctance to travel north had more to do with a fear of being wounded anew should Craig disappoint him than anything else. But no one questioned him, least of all Craig who knew that he had no right to press the point as long as he was with his lover.

The following spring Craig found himself suddenly single again, left by his lover for a younger, non-kinky partner who would be easier to control when absent. Shocked at first by the dissolution of the relationship, Craig later discovered that he was more relieved than anything else. He wrote to Jon and told him, but made no plans to see Jon again though he was now free to seek him out whenever he wished.

He didn't want Jon to think that he'd kept Jon on line for just such an event, and while he wondered if this in fact might be half true, he kept to his decision.

It was not until the anniversary of their meeting in June, when Jon, feeling nostalgic for those few hours spent with Craig the year before, stopped telling Craig about his sexual adventures in his letters (all true, but told, just the same, so that Craig would never feel any obligation to Jon's devotion) and instead begged to see Craig again, to serve him as he had before.

"I've worked hard at the gym since you saw me last," Jon wrote, "to be more worthy of you." He neglected to say that his nipples had been pierced again (once removed soon after Ben's death as a personal sign of mourning) to symbolize his rebirth at Craig's firm hand.

Pleased with the letter, Craig wrote back, telling Jon to be prepared on a weekend in July. Further instructions would be forthcoming. Jon received the letter and was elated. Confident but not foolish, he made discreet inquiries at his office about the possibility of transferring to San Francisco, but only of the possibility and in the vaguest terms.

When Jon stepped onto his doorstep on the morning of the much anticipated weekend, a morning that promised no relief from a week long heat wave, he found a small package with a note that had been tossed over the security gate during the night. Inside was an oversized dog collar, two inches wide and covered with pyramid studs, a D-ring in front. Jon held the collar close to his heart and read the note:

Tonight. Midnight. Cuffs. Wear the collar.

The love that Jon had felt for Craig but had held back, now overflowed. The dam broke. Jon looked at the two muttly dogs that had been Ben's and were now his. "How do you think you'd like living in San Francisco?" he asked them. "It's a lot cooler there." The dogs only panted in the heat, but wagged their tails as they always did when Jon spoke gently to them.

Even as midnight approached, the dessert heat continued. An occasional breeze could be felt, but the sweat continued rolling off of Jon as he drove down Hyperion Boulevard with all the car windows open. He wore his sleaziest pair of Levis, worn and torn in all the right places, a harness, a band on his right arm, and boots. And the collar.

He arrived early but waited until midnight to enter. Sweating as much from anticipation as from the heat, his jeans clung to him with sweat and beads of perspiration covered his brow as he entered the steamy heat of the bar.

Jon felt many pairs of eyes on him as he made his way through the crowd on the small floor. Stray hands wandered over his slick, hairy body. Jon's eyes were fixed on Craig on the far side of the room. He stood directly in front of Craig, his arms at his sides, staring into Craig's handsome, now bearded, face. After several long moments, Craig acknowledged Jon with a nod and a motion to approach. Jon knelt and waited. Craig said nothing for several minutes, only put his booted foot in Jon's crotch, as if to reserve this particular piece of man flesh for his own personal use.

After what seemed like a long time, Craig put down his drink and pulled a leash from his back pocket. Jon's face beamed with pride as the leash was attached to his collar. Craig leaned over and kissed him. Jon felt again the same thirst for Craig's kisses, for Craig's hand on his skin, as before. Then, with only a nod to encourage him, Jon buried his face in Craig's boots, felt his dick strain against his well worn jeans as a gloved hand smacked his ass. Several minutes later Craig led Jon out of the bar on his leash.

Hours passed in what seemed like minutes that night. Once in Craig's hotel room, Jon stripped and was tied to the bed. The door was left open so others could watch, many of them hoping to be invited in to participate, as they cruised the corridors of the hotel. Jon felt the whip and many hands against his skin that night. Many men fucked him, a pile of used rubbers growing by the bedside. Each cock pounded his fuckhole, forcing the cum from his balls. His prostate exploded from the repeated assaults and huge cum stain covered half of the sheet. But only Craig was allowed to kiss him, to hold him and speak gently to him as hot wax was poured over his skin. Jon was in heaven.

Finally Craig shut the door to the room, pushed the men watching the scene away, but left the window open so the watchers could still see them in the gray light of the early morning. Craig fucked Jon for the third time that night, egging Jon on with his words to come one last time, to come with him.

"Shoot it, baby. Shoot it for Daddy. Daddy wants to see you come..."

Jon managed another load, small but forceful, that sent his balls into agony. They collapsed into each other's arms, exhausted. Craig took only a moment to pull the shade and they fell asleep amid the rank and sweat of the sheets, content.

Just as he fell off to sleep he heard Craig whisper, "I love you." He heard it clear enough to know it was not a dream. He wanted to say something, but instead, too quickly, he fell asleep. Hours later Jon woke up being fucked by Craig again. "I love you!" Craig shouted. "Do you hear me? I love you!"

"Kiss me, sir, please. I love you, too."

A short while later, Jon fell asleep in Craig's arms. Jon smiled to himself, felt the same calm certainty he had felt with Ben all those years before. Before he fell back to sleep he fingered the collar locked around his throat and thought to himself, "I'm home."

BAYING AT THE MOON

...And shall you, gliding in your silken shirt,
Deny the hidden bruises of your flesh,
Not boast the livid honour of your hurt?
Come; if they fade, I'll brand you deep afresh.

– V. Sackville-West

New England is dotted with small towns like this one, villages with empty factories and warehouses that were once the centers of their economies, empty brick buildings set along rivers and shore lines, buildings converted to shopping centers, offices, and loft apartments with startling views of New England sweeping past village scenes of churches, storefronts, centuries-old houses, markets, and schools – silver-blue winters, burnt-orange autumns, the oppressive green of summer, the brilliant yellow light of spring: Views from homes like ours.

I watch him in our kitchen while I'm supposed to be working, watch him move with cool efficiency as he chops, slices, grates, tastes, stirs and smells. He is manly as he does these things, as I never knew a man could be in a kitchen. I admire him as he goes about his business, calm and collected, confident. I watch him and smile, content with my life. After so many near misses, after too many tears, we are together.

He looks at me, smiles.

"You're not done, are you, Sir?"

"No, not yet," I answer.

He shakes his head, not daring to chastise me, nor wanting to.

"They'll be here before you know it."

"They" are our dinner guests, people he's collected in the few years of our life here: The women who own the antique store down the road, the Unitarian minister and her husband, the gay biker couple in the next village, Jake and his new Dutch boyfriend, the mayor and her historian husband. They're combined presence will mean activity, noise and conversation. I know he's right and that I should get back to it.

"And you want that grant."

"This is my grant proposal, not yours, boy."

He beams.

"Yes, Sir."

As usual, those two words give me an instant hard-on. I'm tempted to order him to suck my cock then and there, knowing that he'd obey me in an instant, eager, smiling and without question. But I also know that this interruption might interfere with his preparations, leading him to apologize for a meal that falls short of his expectations. He would apologize repeatedly, blaming only himself, even when it was my interruption that caused the shortcomings of the meal, shortcomings apparent only to him.

So I only smile instead. Going back to my work I realize once again that I am, as I am everyday, happier than I was even a moment before.

×××

Barry was dancing the first time I saw him. He was also probably high, he tells me now. Jake and I were at the Pleasure Dome after the Folsom Street Fair, and Barry was in the center of the dance floor, moving his whole body in time to the music, arms above his head, eyes closed, oblivious to me and the world. He wore calf-high boots and worn Levis undone at the waist. He was shirtless, a thick chain locked around his neck that I didn't understand the meaning of despite all the boys in collars and on leashes I'd seen that day, not even when Sam (red-bearded and as hairy as me) pulled on that chain and locked Barry in a kiss that lasted uncounted minutes, a kiss I watched with awe and envy.

"He's a beauty all right," Jake yelled in my ear over the din of the music.

"What's with the necklace?" I asked my friend.

"He's the other man's slave."

Hearing those words I was more in wonder than before, more in lust with the lithe, sweaty body, its muscles accentuated by just enough hair (almost as blond as the rest of him) to make him man enough for me. His fair beard, like Sam's, was full but carefully groomed, his hair buzzed short. I ached (yes, that is the word) to kiss him, to hold him. I wanted my seed in him. I wanted to mark him as mine.

"Then he's definitely taken?" I asked Jake, trying to make a light of my pain and disappointment.

Jake laughed, not sensing the storm of lust and frustration raging inside me.

"Yeah, Joey, I think so. But as usual, we've both spotted the perfect *shegetz*."

"I'm a *shegetz*," I reminded my friend.

"You're Italian, Joe. That doesn't count."

This was (and is) an old joke between us, and we laughed as always.

×××

Jake and I have been best friends since third grade. He told me he liked guys (and was in love with a waspy beauty he played tennis with) while we were still in high school. Ten years later I told him that I also loved men. Fortunately for us – or maybe unfortunately – we always like the same guys (blond icebergs, Jake calls them), so there was never any question of our being lovers, only of competing for the same guys.

"You're sure about this, Joe?" Jake asked me when I told him that my marriage had been a mistake, that I'd fallen in love with another intern, my handsome Nordic Todd. "You're not just doing this to be fashionable?"

"Yeah, Jake. I'm just doing it so I can be closer to you, faggot."

"Who're you calling faggot?"

"I'm calling me a faggot. And I figure if I'm going to be a faggot, I can at least be a man about it."

Which is when Jake hugged me, like I had hugged him ten years before. And we kissed each other on the cheek as we had done then and ever since.

×××

"You're such warm people," my Danish wife once commented when she saw our usual embrace. Her voice had the same tone of disappointment and disapproval it had when she discovered that I was Italian rather than Jewish and why the Jew she was flirting with that night at the student coffee shop would not respond to her. Had I not loved her as much as I did, I suppose I'd have been too hurt to be her second choice, but she was so beautiful that I was flattered to be just that – until I met Todd and he turned my life upside down with a single kiss.

×××

Jake and I danced together the rest of that night, or until it was time to hit Blow Buddies. As we danced, I watched Barry dancing without stop, his face beatific. I watched while the sweat made tiny rivers down his torso to form a damp spot at his crotch, and down his back to form another one in the ass crack of his Levis. I wanted bury my face in his ass, to lick up the sweat and inhale his scent.

He was like some great cat, a lion basking in the pleasure of the music, in the shifting lights surrounding him, in my admiration, in his Master's love. Yes, he was the cat, content and laying in the sun: I was a dog, alone in the darkness, howling at the moon and afraid I'd never attain the thing I wanted most to love.

I shot my load so many times that night at Blow Buddies, each time thinking of the still nameless beauty dancing half-naked with his Master and never noticing me. Every mouth I kissed I pretended was his. But imagination can only take a man so far.

I flew back to Boston the next afternoon and life went on as before. Except when I jerked-off and fanaticized about him, about his kiss and the feel of my dick in his mouth or butt hole. Other than those moments alone, I forgot about him. Instead I searched for love among the men I met at home, always accepting lust when love wasn't offered.

×××

"You're husband material," Jake, ever the amateur therapist, said a few months after I told him I was gay. "That's why you got married so young. Some men are lovers and some men are husbands. Most men are one before becoming the other. But you're a husband by temperament. Like me. We'll take sex, but we want love."

After I got back from San Francisco, I asked him during one of our frequent phone conversations what he thought about Masters and slaves, about Dads and boys.

"It's an intense kind of intimacy, Joe. Why? You think you might be into it? After what we saw, I'm not surprised. Leather looks damn hot."

"I keep wondering what its appeal is. And, yeah, it turns me on."

"Then explore it," he said. I could almost hear his mischievous smile. "I am."

It's great having a best buddy who gives you permission to be yourself.

×××

The next summer in Provincetown, I saw Barry again. And again he was dancing, bare-chested and chained, with his Master. Again I watched them kiss, watched in desperate wonder at their shared passion. Again he didn't notice me.

After the bars closed I went down to the docks and slapped around a boy who almost reminded me of my nameless beauty, slapped him around and pulled on the chain locked around his neck as I fucked his face. He accepted my cum gratefully, then asked me to fuck his ass. I was happy to comply, but I knew it wasn't the same as having a boy of my own.

When we were done, I asked him where he was from.

"San Francisco."

"I should've known. All the hot bottoms are from there."

He laughed. "Thanks."

"What's your name?"

"Matt. I'm here with my Owner."

I was startled by the carelessness with which he said this.

"Does he know you're here?"

"He's over there," Matt nodded to a particularly dark and busy corner, a cluster of moving shadows filled with grunts and groans, with murmured promises that would fade at the first hint of light.

"You're so casual about these things out West."

Matt shrugged.

"I guess."

Then he kissed me and reached for my cock, already hardening again.

"Up for another round?" he asked with a crooked smile, handing me another condom.

How I wanted someone to smile at me like that all the time, to look at me as Barry looked at Sam. As always, I took what I could get. When I shot my third load I looked up at the moon, full and heavy, half hidden in the clouds of a coming storm, and howled.

×××

I did my best to forget about him. And for while I did. Then, a few years later, Jake and I headed to London for what had become our annual vacation together, as usual sharing a hotel room but not a bed. Every night Jake and I took a black cab to the leather bars.

And, yes, there he was again. This time he was being led around the Hoist on a leash by his Master, licking the boots of strangers. I put myself in their way so that my beautiful man, my nameless beauty, would lick my boots. They approached and I met Sam's eye. We nodded, and there he was, Barry, groveling at my booted feet. I put one boot behind his neck while he licked the other. Eventually he made his way past my boots to my leather pants, and then to the codpiece. I looked at Sam and he nodded, signaling me to unleash my fat cock from the leather codpiece and let it find its home in the deep, warm, wet throat waiting for it.

I looked back down at Barry, at his eager mouth grasping the codpiece between its teeth, his eyes looking up at me for permission. I nodded and he pulled it loose. My cock burst out of its confines, fast and furious, slapping him across the face. He let out a small cry of surprise to see the size of it, but opened wide without a second's hesitation. It was even better than I'd imagined, more wonderful than I'd dared hope. His mouth engulfed me. I was swallowed whole and I cried out to know such pleasure, such beauty. I put one hand behind his head and fucked.

Sam drew closer, caressed my pierced nipples through the thick hair that covers my entire chest and torso, and kissed me. Our beards met before our tongues, igniting the space between us. Even as we kissed, I screamed to the ceiling – and came. Cum shot out of me in thick streams. I could feel it explode from the very base of my balls. Ribbon after ribbon spurted out of me, all greedily swallowed by my nameless beauty, the perfect vehicle for my seed.

Sam finished kissing me, and I pulled Barry to his feet. Finally, for the first time, I kissed him. After aching for that kiss for so long, it was an even bigger release than cumming down his throat had been. To hold him at last, to feel the softness of his lips and the bristle of his stubble-length beard, was the purest joy I'd known until that moment.

When are lips parted, Sam was standing there smiling.

"Hey, thanks, buddy."

"Yes. Thank you, Sir."

"Sure, pal." I nodded to his slave. "Boy."

"You're American like us?"

"Afraid so."

"Then let me buy you one."

Yes, the camaraderie of Americans meeting abroad. We introduced ourselves. I found out that they were from Chicago, that Sam's work allowed them to travel a lot, and that my beloved boy's name was Barry. Barry said little, letting his Master speak most of the time. But he smiled a lot, and whenever his eyes met mine, I saw pleasure in them, pleasure in his subtle smile, like the cat lying in a patch of sunlight and lifting its face to better enjoy the sensation of the sun's warmth. I didn't tell them that I'd seen them in San Francisco and Provincetown, that I'd wanted Barry for years, that I envied what they had. I only exchanged email addresses knowing I'd never contact them for fear I'd make a fool of myself should I ever see them again, should I should ever see Barry again.

I went back to the hotel before Jake did and jerked-off I don't know how many times thinking of Barry. His mouth was so incredible; I could only wonder how good his fuckhole must feel. I wanted it but didn't dare hope for it. Once again, I was alone in the night, baying at the distant, unattainable moon. But it was a moon I'd now been to, a moon warm and beautiful and fantastically familiar, a moon that might perhaps be within my reach.

×××

After that I fucked and flogged men whenever I could: Men who said they were boys, boys who thought they were men, hot bottoms who wanted to please me and wear my collar for the weekend but to live their own lives from Monday to Friday, men who wanted only the one night and no more, men without any sense self who wanted to immolate themselves on mine, and hopeful hungry slaves hoping to hook me as their Master/husband and so land the plum role of doctor's wife. This last group disgusted me. I wanted my man to be my boy, yes, and to own him; but I also wanted him to be his own man, capable of self-sufficiency; or of what value would be the gift of his person to me? I had no real sense yet of what I wanted that man to be, other than my ideal of Barry, but I knew that he would not be a wife. I'd had a wife already, and I didn't want another one, of either sex.

I also learned that whatever pleasure and pain might be shared with these men, when there was no heart connection, no sense of mutual regard, affection or respect, there was no satisfaction either. It didn't matter how sweet his ass was, how deep he could inhale my cock down his throat, how much pain he could take from a single-tail whip, or how I made him scream: If we didn't care about each other, at least a little, I didn't care about the sex. How much more wonderful it would be, I imagined, when I found the man/boy of my own, the one I could love forever?

×××

Fast-forward a few more years: I was in Chicago with (of course) Jake. Jake had just broken-up with another boyfriend, so we headed to the Steamworks. Nothing like plentiful anonymous sex to ease the pain of lost love, we figured.

I hadn't been there a few minutes it seemed, when I found myself surrounded by a bevy of big blonde Midwesterners, kissing them, feeling my ass being eaten, my pits licked, my nipples chewed, my cock sucked. I gave myself over to the flood of sensation, eyes closed and happier than I'd been in a while. Then I heard a grunt, a groan, and a sigh that told me – what? I don't know, but I opened my eyes and looked out the door of the room we were in and across the hall into a room with a sling. A man was stepping away from the sling, shaking his spent dick of excess juice, stepping aside to reveal who was in the sling: My angel: Barry. Our eyes met.

I shook off my cluster of farm boys (as I'd dubbed them) for the one whose fuckhole I'd longed for for so many years, longed for almost as much as I had for his kiss. I shut the door behind me, smiled, and stepped up to the sling, to the sweet hole puckered and ready for me to fuck.

I reached for a condom.

"Fuck me raw."

"No, I can't. I won't."

"Yes you can. The others did. It's all right."

"No it's not, Barry."

At the sound of his name, he looked up at me and, recognizing me for the first time, started to tremble. I saw tears in the corners of his eyes. To quiet him, I leaned over to kiss him, to comfort him. Then I noticed that there was no collar around his neck. Something was very wrong. I pulled him out of the sling, held him close.

"Come on," I whispered.

I laid him down on the mattress and held him close, kissing away the manly tears, caressing the hard, hairy body I wanted to know every inch of, to study for years to come.

"He's dead, you know."

"Sam?"

"Yeah. Master died in that plane crash last summer. I was supposed to join him in Paris a few days later. And…"

"It's okay, boy. I understand."

"Do you? Do you know how I feel? Do you know how it feels not to care if you live or die?"

"We've all lost loved ones, boy," I said, perhaps too severely. "As much as you hurt, you don't have a monopoly on pain."

He was quiet a moment, looked into my eyes and reached up with his mouth for a kiss that I was glad to give him. Then his hand reached for my cock.

"I want you to fuck me."

I reached for a condom. He didn't resist this time. I lifted his legs onto my own strong shoulders, and entered paradise.

"Oh, baby…"

"Sir?"

"Oh, baby, baby…"

"You like it, Sir?"

Not since Matt under the pier in Provincetown had I met a man who could grab my dick with his fuckhole like Barry was doing now. He squeezed on my cock, then relaxed his hold on me, varying the tautness of his hole with the intensity of my strokes. This was not a passive bottom that lay still, expecting to be pleased. This was a man who sought to please his partner with all the skill he could muster, with at least as much skill as most of the men who fucked him must have offered him that night.

"Baby, baby, it feels so good. It's so fucking amazing, boy, it's so fucking incredible."

And then he did that thing he does, that thing I have no words for and can't describe, that sent me over the edge, screaming into the abyss of orgasm. I shouted so loud that there was a sudden pause in the constant chatter of the bathhouse beyond our little room, a stunned silence followed by nervous laughter and knowing guffaws. I collapsed on top of him, our bodies colliding, slick with sweat.

"Baby."

"Sir."

I almost said, "I love you" but didn't dare. Even if it was true.

We kept fucking, each of us cumming time after time. He was focused on me, and I on him. We were our own little world, an eternal moment that could never be repeated or lost now that we were together. Or so I told myself, so I hoped he felt as well.

I bent him over my knee to spank him between fucks, twisted his nipples, then held him down as I raped his hole, spat in his face, but never stopped kissing him.

At some point I heard Jake calling my name, and realized that we would have to end it sometime.

"I never want to let you go."

"I don't want you to, either, Sir."

"Are you ready for that?"

"Master has been dead more than a year, Sir. It's time I decided."

I kissed him again, losing myself once more in the softness of his lips, in the bristle of his beard.

Jake called my name again.

"Come on, boy. Let me introduce you to my best buddy in the world."

×××

Four in the morning found the three of us at a diner on Halsted eating lousy burgers and trading tales.

"You don't remember the first time I saw you, Barry."

"Yes, I do."

"You think it was in London, but you're wrong. It was at the Pleasure Dome in San Francisco, right after the Folsom Street Fair. You were dancing with Sam and I thought you were the handsomest man I'd ever seen. We both did. Ask Jake. He was there."

Barry shook his head.

"I don't remember seeing you there, but I was probably high. It was years before that, though. You don't remember? It was in high school."

"Not in Wakefield? Wakefield, Massachusetts?"

"Ayah. You were a year ahead of me. And I had such a crush on you. But I also thought you two were lovers and I used to follow you around hoping to see the two of you kiss, just so I'd know I wasn't the only queer in town."

Jake laughed.

"You weren't. Trust me."

"One time you were shooting hoops at the park and you caught me watching you through the fence and one of you asked if I wanted to join the game. I was scared shitless and ran. But later I always wished I'd gone in and played ball with you guys."

"That was you?"

Barry nodded.

"Yes, Sir. And when we saw you in London, I recognized you immediately – even with the beard you had then. I was so glad to finally get to touch you. Master said I could suck one dick that wasn't his that night. And I'd wanted yours for so long."

"Synchronicity," I murmured half-aloud, in wonder that our mutual longings should have lasted all these years.

"*Beshert!*" Jake said with sudden finality. "It was meant to be!"

×××

Our courtship progressed slowly, if steadily. We both knew where we were going, that we were heading for the same destination, and we took our time getting there. We traveled back and forth, Barry more than me, and spent every available holiday and vacation together.

Sam's death had left Barry financially fixed, if rudderless. His mourning had turned into depression that devolved into a self-destructive spiral. Occasional drug use became a constant, and unprotected sex with strangers the norm. By some miracle, he avoided infection or worse. Sometimes he credits me for bringing him out of the miasma of his pain, but that's a gross exaggeration. All I did was appear at the moment when he was ready to bring his life back into focus.

"Synchronicity," I tell him.

"*Beshert!*" he responds.

Now that he didn't need to work, he could do what he really wanted, which was to go to graduate school, to study and teach. He applied to schools all over New England thinking he'd attend the school closest to me and Boston. Then, on one of his weeklong visits (a week he spent collared, often naked, periodically flogged or whipped, and occasionally chained), I told him that I'd been offered a job at a teaching hospital in New Hampshire. He looked at me strangely.

"Where in New Hampshire, Sir?"

I told him.

"They just accepted me into grad school, Sir."

"Is it where you want to go, boy?"

"Yes, Sir. It was my first choice," he said. "Synchronicity."

"No," I corrected him. "*Beshert!*"

×××

I woke up this morning to find him next to me, awake, sitting on the edge of the bed and looking out the window at the slowly moving river this former factory was once dependent on for power and transportation. I reached over, touched him, and he turned to me with his usual smile.

"Sir," is all he said, all he ever needs to say.

I pulled him to me, kissed him hard, held him tight, spread his legs and fucked him through the convenient hole in the back of the union suit he wears to bed during our New England winters, fucked him without so much as spit between us. He opened to accept me, opened then squeezed tight. Now that he's mine, now that he wears my collar, he is where I plant my seed. That's how I mark him as mine. I do what no one else is allowed to do. The collar is only the symbol.

×××

I think of how my wife had demanded my help on occasions like this. She was, quite naturally, demanding equality in our marriage, something Barry neither wants nor needs. His self-confidence and my belief in him are all that matters, that and the chain around his neck and my seed in his body. We are two orbs circling each other, reflecting our love back and forth, two planets dancing in perfect sync.

Just before our guests arrive he showers and puts on a fresh shirt. Then, because there is time, and because I need it, he sucks my cock, successfully drawing the cum from my balls just moments before the doorbell rings. As always, his timing is impeccable.

At dinner, the local historian again remarks that one of the town's founding families shared Barry's surname. Barry's response to this information is polite interest. He knows already that he is their descendent but refuses to take credit or blame for this accident of birth.

"You're such a great cook," the minister's husband remarks. "It's almost enough to make me want to be gay. Honey, why don't you cook like this?"

His wife shakes her head and roles her eyes, this being a tender point between them.

The women with the antique store laugh, delighted to watch the foibles of their heterosexual neighbors. The biker couple shares a smirk with each other and us.

"That's not fair," Barry says with his usual modesty. "Cooking is just a hobby for me. And I don't have a congregation to respond to at all hours. Besides, we eat very simply most of the time. Often it's just soup and bread."

"True," I agree, not saying that the soup is one he makes himself, the bread fresh because he's learning the art of baking it, that canned and frozen food are a rarity in our kitchen unless prepared by him. No one knows the trouble he goes to when he cooks, or how well we live. Like all New Englanders, he likes it that way, the exact details of his personal life kept a mystery.

I smile at him, prouder than ever, my cock hardening again

×××

I watch Barry the next afternoon working at his desk, absentmindedly petting the cat that sits next to the keyboard, purring. I fucked and flogged him the night before as a reward for a successful dinner party. Then fucked him again this morning, making sure he shot his own load before I gave him mine. He hums as he strokes his cat, content with the warmth of the healing welts on his back, with the feeling of my seed deep in his guts, with the touch of his cat's winter coat. Then he notices me watching him and starts to stand up.

"Sir?"

"Its okay, babe. Just admiring my boy."

"Your boy who's turning gray, Sir."

"As if that could make me love you less."

He laughs, crossing the room to my chair where I've been working on my grant proposal, and sits at my feet. I stroke his short hair and beard, happier than ever to have captured my mysterious other in the crook of my heart. He leans his head against my leg to better appreciate my touch and sighs deeply, tendering a kiss to my free hand.

Together we watch Barry's cat stretch, jump off the desk, stretch again, and step noiselessly across the carpet to our dog laying in a patch of winter sunlight, absorbing what warmth he can from it. The dog lifts his head to the cat's soft salutation, to the gentle touch of the cat's paw on his muzzle. They touch noses in greeting before a brief but well-mannered exchange of affectionate grooming, and the cat curls himself up with the dog, purring loudly.

The dog wags his tail, content.

POZ2POZ,
OR,
EROS ON A SUMMER NIGHT

Chastity and loneliness are one and the same misfortune.

– Colette

He didn't look exactly like the photo I'd seen online, but none of us do.

We all post the most flattering pictures we can take of ourselves, the ones that show us as we think others will want us, the ones that come closest to showing us how we want to be seen. But I wasn't disappointed. He was fairer than I'd expected, but no less burly. Best of all he was what my friends and I call a GOA: Guy Our Age. That is, he was a grown-up who, like us, was just old enough to remember the sexual abandon that ended so suddenly twenty years before.

As promised, he was also a good kisser. We were in a lip-lock almost at once. Only after several minutes did we separate our mouths from each other's tongues.

"Woof!"

It was a hot, humid summer night. I was alone in Chicago and staying with a old buddy from San Francisco – a buddy who was spending that sticky Friday night with his boyfriend in an air-conditioned apartment across town and leaving me to my own devices. It was one of those nights when the air fairly aches for rain that doesn't come, and I felt just as frustrated as the stifled, unquenched city that night – lonely and horny, and not sure how much of which was making me wrap my arms around the handsome, bearded babe in front of me, both of us wanting the same kind of release.

He said online that he liked to get sweaty, that he liked to fuck for hours, that he liked to fuck raw. Ditto, ditto, and ditto, had been my responses.

"Poz?" he asked, looking for a final confirmation.

"Poz," I affirmed.

"And you want it long and hard?"

"Oh, yeah."

"And you want my loads?"

"Fuck yeah."

"Cool."

Another kiss and we were at each other's clothes, getting naked as quickly as we could. The window let in what little breeze there was into the sparsely furnished bedroom, the sound of traffic from Halsted Street a block away carried clearly to us in the heat of the painfully still night. I knelt down and sucked his cock, fat and healthy and just big enough to hurt a little – because if it doesn't hurt at least a little, he's not doing it right. He was hard in no time. He was ready. So was I.

"How do you like it?"

"Anyway you want to give it to me," I answered truthfully. "But my favorite is laying on my stomach, being held down. I like to struggle and lose."

His eyes fairly lit up in the dark room.

"Woof," he exclaimed again. "You're my kinda guy."

I bent over the bed and pulled his hard, beautiful cock towards my ass. He rubbed it against my hole and I gasped with pleasure. I leaned against the bed. Then it came, that first friction, that first marvelous sensation of being entered. I threw my head back.

"Oh, yeah!"

He pushed slowly inside of me, just spit and sweat for lube. I groaned again, rolling my head back and forth.

"Oh, fuck!" he whispered. "Geezus Fuckin' Fuck!"

He pulled out and pushed back in, then did it again. And again. I was moaning in gratitude, giving myself up to the pleasure of having a man inside me, skin to skin, a man who was going to give me his sweet, hot load: His manhood, his essence, his maleness, his seed.

He pushed me down onto the bed and was on top of me, holding me down while I fought (not to hard) to free myself, feeling the pleasure of finding there was no escape from the hammer strokes ramming inside of me.

"I'm raping your ass, man. I'm fuckin' raping your ass!"

"Yes, Sir!" was all I managed to say. "Oh, yes, Sir…"

He was a jackhammer, pounding my hairy ass, a nonstop power fuck. He fucked better than most porn stars because he was really into it – and into me. The pressure was already building inside him. I could feel it mounting, feel the head of his cock swelling.

"You want my fuckin' load? You want it?"

"Yes, Sir! Please, Sir!"

"You want me to fucking sperm you, cocksucker?"

"Fucking breed me!"

"I'm gonna poz you man! I'm gonna fuckin' poz you!"

"Do it, fucker!"

I felt it happen deep in my hole, felt the explosion, the shaft of his cock pumping his load into my guts. Just as suddenly, I felt complete.

He collapsed on top of me, his sweat pouring over me, and rolled over onto the already damp sheet.

"Man, oh, man! You can really take it!"

"And you know how to give it, mister."

"Hot fuckin' damn!"

"You said it…"

"I'm good for a couple more, you know!"

"Hot fucking damn!"

After he caught his breath, he got up and got us each a glass of cold water.

"You're amazing," he said.

"You're doing all the work!"

"But you're such a great fuck. I keep meeting these party boys who get tired of getting fucked in about ten minutes – or less!"

"Amateurs! Ten minutes or less doesn't count as a fuck," I said.

"Amen to that! And you like it raw, man."

"Call me old fashioned," I said. "But if I don't have a load up my ass, I haven't been fucked."

"Speaking of which," he said reaching for my sweaty, funky fuck hole.

""Fuck me on my back first," I asked. "Just until I cum. Then you can role me over and go to town, hard and heavy as you want."

My feet were in the air, resting on his football player shoulders as he entered me a second time. Again, the initial contact, that first friction, sent my mind reeling. I thrashed beneath him as he sawed away, pumping like a piston, watching me as I jerked-off. I tried to hold back but couldn't. I exploded in a matter of minutes, my load shooting through the air, across my abdomen, shoulders and face, splattering across the sheets.

When, I asked myself, was the last time I came like that? I couldn't remember.

"You still want me to go on? After that?"

"Oh, yeah, fucker. It still feels good."

"Hot damn. You're amazing, man."

He rolled me over, keeping his dick inside me, turning me onto my stomach like a pig on a stick. I almost screamed with pleasure at the sensation, at feeling my fuckhole stroked sideways by his beautiful, fat cock. Then he was pounding away inside me, pounding like the jackhammer he was, unstoppable, insatiable, reaching for a second climax. He lasted a lot longer this time, fucked me longer and harder.

My head was rolling back and forth as I spoke in tongues, as he grunted and groaned and talked a line of filth that made it all the more exciting.

"You're my little fuck pig, aren't you? You want me to rape your fuckin' hole, don't you? You want all my fuckin' ball juice up your ass! You fuckin' want it!"

"Yes, Sir," I heard myself whimper as I gave myself over to wave after wave of pleasure, a nameless joy flowing from deep inside me and radiating like rings in a pond to every fiber of my being, waiting for what I knew would come – again. Every part of me quivered in expectation of his second load.

His words turned into grunts and groans. His cock head swelled as the jackhammer rhythm quickened, as the piston pushed deeper inside me. Then the roar of orgasm, the tensing of his entire body on top of me, the almost audible pumping of his cock as jism spilled itself inside of me.

"Damn!" was all he could say when he'd rolled off of me a second time. "I hope you never wear out."

"I don't," I admitted. "Can't you find a piggy bottom here in Chicago?"

"Not like you!"

"Funny, hot tops like you are hard to find in San Francisco. And when I find one, he's always an import. I always look for guys from the Midwest. They're the best tops."

He laughed, not understanding how sincere I was.

More water, more talking.

We licked the sweat off of each other; lay in the street-lit darkness of his bedroom, listening to the ceaseless midnight motion of Chicago beyond the window.

"Here," he said after a while. "Lay on your side and let me spoon you."

I obeyed and felt him enter me for the third time. I groaned softly as he pushed in and out of me, rolled my head and pushed my butt back against his groin. A moment later I was on my stomach again and the jackhammer had returned, rearranging my guts with his cock, prodding and poking my insides looking for that magic button that would make me scream. And then he found it, hitting my prostate dead on. He heard me yelp in pleasure and pain, heard me and responded by hammering away at that one spot for as long as he could, pummeling it (and me) with the most intense sensation I'd felt in years, pleasure that increased from plateau to plateau. I didn't even feel him approach his climax this time, so lost was I in my own. But then his cock head was swelling again. As it gushed cum for the third time, I shot my second load against the damp sheets. We roared as one into the still, humid darkness as we came, called out to the nameless god of the orgasm in gratitude for the momentary ecstasy that falls just short of love.

It was a while before either of us could talk, a while before either of us could think clearly enough to form words.

"Geezus!"

"Damn!"

"I've never…"

"No. Not like that."

He leaned over and kissed me. We kissed deeply for several glorious minutes in the after glow of that amazing orgasm, our bodies still trembling with delight.

"Thanks," was all he said before collapsing back onto the sweaty, funky sheets.

The whole room smelled of man sex, of sweat and cum. How I wanted to stay there forever, lost in the haze of our hormones and mutual pleasure. But it was late, and I knew better. This sort of sex, this brilliant a fuck, can never be repeated. We would never be lovers, we both knew, not living in different cities as we did. And hardly knowing each other, the intimacy of this moment, the mere memory of it, would be unbearable when we awoke. A morning together, another fuck, would only be a disappointment.

It was three o'clock in the morning when I kissed him goodbye and rambled slowly through Boys Town and back to my buddy's empty apartment in Lakeview, a twenty-minute walk spent being with and by myself. My hardened widower's heart felt soft and tender again in the concrete and neon darkness of the city streets. I asked myself how long this new softness would last: Long enough to fall in love again?

Jizz leaked out of my fuckhole, oozed past my khaki shorts and down my bare legs as I walked through the almost deserted streets. It felt dirty and wonderful, so wrong and so right. I could only smirk with satisfaction as cum trickled down my calf and reached my other wise pristine white sock. I felt like a cat with milk on his whiskers, like a dog wagging his tail after belching.

I was startled from my reverie by the sudden crash of thunder and an equally sudden burst of cooling rain a moment later. I looked up to the sky to feel a new kind of sensual pleasure: A face full of summer rain.

The night was complete.

DAMAGED

Fantasy is toxic: the private cruelty and the world war
both have their start in the human brain.

– Elizabeth Bowen

It was generally agreed that the initial impact of the bus' side view mirror hadn't caused Kevin's temporary loss of memory, but rather the second blow to the head when he landed on the sidewalk. The first force only caused the concussion; it was the cracking of his head on the cement that knocked years from his memory. Which collision (either with concrete or with stainless steel) would have the profoundest affect on Kevin's future, by impairing any ability to experience his former passions, was merely a matter of speculation.

Kevin woke up in the hospital and knew at once where he was, and that he must have been in an accident of some kind if he was getting a sponge bath while heavily bandaged and aching all over – even if he had no memory of the Chicago Transit Authority's assault, nor of how his head had ricocheted from one hard surface to the next; or even of how he'd spent the last few days. It was only when he saw Lee standing at the foot of the bed, that Kevin showed anything approaching confusion.

"Who are you?"

"I'm Lee. We live together. We had a wedding last summer in my parents' backyard. Remember?"

"No. Are you trying to put one over on me?"

Lee pulled out his wallet and showed Kevin the picture of the two of them holding hands, both in morning suits, in a suburban backyard.

"For real?" was Kevin's only response.

Doctor's were called, questions asked of Kevin – questions to which he no longer knew the answers: *What year was it? Who was the president of the United States? What was his address?*

Looking at his driver's license, Kevin saw that, indeed, it was the same address as the one on Lee's license. He was also surprised to see that his hairline had receded and that he'd grown a beard.

No I haven't given you the expected descriptions of their god-like beauty, chiseled features, huge cocks and perfect bodies. This is because these details are irrelevant to the tale being told –as well as untrue. But, you, The Common Reader, want to know these things: You want to be assured that the men you're imagining are worth getting hard for, worth thinking about as you rearrange your crotch. Suffice it to say that Kevin is fair and Irish while Lee is dark and Welsh, and that they had, until this moment, shared that peculiar Celtic sensibility of taking a joy in life (which is to say, an acute pleasure in food, drink, music, telling tales, fighting, dancing and making love) with a passion normally associated with Mediterranean peoples. Both are furry and over thirty, though Lee is a few years senior. They are burly men who work out together several days a week, and if they were the type of men one was looking for online, one would call them Muscle Bears. Their beards might change with the seasons and the fashions, but they are always bearded and know that they are kind of men who are the handsomer for it.

"Sometimes these things happen," offered the nurse, a small brown woman with an indeterminate accent. "Memories usually come back in a few days. Do you want to see your mother now, Kevin? She's waiting outside."

"Hell no! If that bitch is here, you better call security because she is not supposed to be anywhere near me. There's a restraining order!" Kevin turned to Lee for confirmation. "That's still true, isn't it?"

"Yup. And it goes for both of us."

"But she's your mother…"

"She also arranged to have me kidnapped so I could be held captive by some charlatan who promised he'd make me straight – but only after he'd taken all of her money, of course. Ask her yourself, if you want to. She'll be happy to tell you about her Christian duty."

"If you don't call security, I will," added Lee firmly.

The nurse hesitated, once more offering the information that the woman sitting in the hall with her well-worn Bible was Kevin's mother, so Lee reached for the phone as the nurse shook her head in disbelief. A few minutes later Kevin's mother could be heard screaming in the hallway: Threats of legal action, God's wrath, and the newspapers being informed of this outrage were all proffered with no effect. Lee smiled to hear the theatrically maternal cries of moral outrage, then turned back to Kevin expecting to see the same smug satisfaction on his partner's face but saw instead two empty eyes that registered no pleasure in once again frustrating his mother's martyrdom, but only a dull dismay at the depth of the disturbed woman's emotion.

Friends came to visit Kevin in the hospital. Photo albums and mementos were proffered. Stories were told of Kevin and Lee's life together. Bit by bit memories were recovered and Kevin's lost years were pieced together. His college years, his courtship with Lee, his teaching second grade in Highland Park, all came back, but elicited no feeling from him. Always passionate about food, and with very particular likes and dislikes, he now ate whatever was put before him when he was hungry, and then lost interest in eating when his stomach no longer felt empty. Always fond of children and animals, the mere thought of either now made him anxious and uneasy. His shared passion with Lee (fucking first thing in the morning and the last thing at night with the addition, when possible, of matinees and pre-dinner romps), that had been the envy of all, was now like a withered ear of corn, a dried husk with no fruit within it. Television provided no diversion in the hospital, offering only noise and confusing images; even his favorite old movies meant nothing to him.

When he came home, Kevin turned to books, the ones he had loved since he was a child growing up in southern Illinois. He started with the Oz books, once forbidden to him by his parents and (and so, as a child, read only at the library), the complete collection of which were now his pride and joy.

The books he brought home had been examined with suspicion by his parents. No fairy tales, science fiction or fantasy, were allowed. Encyclopedia Brown, Tornado Jones, Henry Huggins and the Hardy Boys were grudgingly approved. Later came Laura Ingles Wilder, Louisa May Alcott, Jack London and Mark Twain, and finally his favorite, Charles Dickens, all of them passing before his parents' ever persistent scrutiny. The Chronicles of Prydain and Narnia, along with Ray Bradbury's books and J.R.R. Tolkien's tomes, he hid in his school locker, only reading them in the homes of friends.

With sudden regularity, one or both of his parents would burst into his bedroom, accusation livid in their eyes as they pulled whatever he was reading from his hands, followed by their sullen disappointment at finding neither pornography nor self-abuse under their roof – both of which Kevin sensibly confined to deserted barns with his equally frustrated friends. Staying a few steps ahead of his parents, he took an easy pleasure in their frustration.

×××

Now he read again the books he remembered loving, and in the comfort of familiar fiction he experienced something approaching pleasure. As the tales unraveled, as the characters' lives evolved through each story, he found a singular solace in the otherwise empty universe he had come to inhabit.

Sex with Lee had become mechanical and only about orgasm, one more task to be completed. Only when he was fucked did he find some lasting pleasure; the complex chemistry of his lover's cum becoming a permanent part of him elevated his mood, sent into his bloodstream an endorphin-like release from an existence that was otherwise without affect. Alone in bed and dripping semen as his husband showered, he felt something like satisfaction: Only then did he smile.

Unable to work, Kevin spent his days visiting psychiatrists, neurologists, social workers, attorneys, numerous therapists, the offices of his former Union, and numerous government agencies to secure the needed income. Somewhere amidst his daily travels between and around Lake View and the Loop, it occurred to him that he could go to the baths. There he could again be fucked and again (since intimacy played no part in the primal joy that came from it) feel the same completion. Though he and Lee had until then been nominally monogamous, he paid his membership and went in without a second thought. The halls were not as crowded as he'd hoped, but there were enough men (and he was not so choosy about them any more than he was about his diet) to provide the needed injection of cum; with more cum came more of the required chemistry. He felt better, almost happy, but ached for the euphoria he remembered once feeling in Lee's arms, legs, cock and buttocks.

It was also in the baths that he rediscovered pornography and found that the visual of other men fucking was comforting as well as arousing, and the lack of plot a requisite for his being able to concentrate on what he watched. In the pornography he found online he discovered what he most wanted to see: A single man being fucked by many men until he dripped semen, a beatific smile across the bottom's face. To be like that man, to be the man more men would want to leave their seed in, he took a renewed interest in his own appearance. He cut his hair short and trimmed his beard to little more than stubble. Now much thinner, he returned to the gym and firmed the farm-trained musculature waiting beneath his formerly *zaftig* frame. Almost everyday he douched and went to one of the local bathhouses, got fucked and felt better. If Kevin was absent when Lee came home from work, Lee made his own dinner, walked the dog, and was happy to see Kevin looking so much better when he eventually came home with vague tales of losing track of the time. Lee was even happier to find Kevin was now eager for sex, or at least to get fucked, for only then was there anything like tenderness between them.

Until Lee woke up one morning with the clap, that is. At that moment everything Lee had suspected but denied came together with one final furious wave. He screamed at Kevin, whose impassive face drove him to distraction, yelled accusations that were only acknowledged with nods of agreement. Kevin denied nothing for he felt no remorse for his actions, but was, in fact, more intrigued than worried by Lee's outrage. It was not until Lee's hurt drove him to strike Kevin hard across the face in some final retaliation that Kevin felt anything at all. Pain, he realized at that moment, led to a pleasant release in it's subsiding. If the pain were greater, so would the subsequent release from it: Just as every action had a reaction, so pain led to pleasure.

Frustrated at Kevin's lack of response, Lee stormed out and Kevin calmly went online looking for an apartment. By the time Lee returned to their condominium (looking over downtown Chicago because Lake views were static, even dull, to their shared Celtic aesthetic), Kevin had packed what he deemed necessary and left, moving into a shabby little apartment a block off of Halsted Street. He now had the settlement from his accident and his disability checks to live on. Still able to feel guilt, or at least discomfort, at having caused Lee such distress (though not enough to make any amends to his husband, only enough to remove himself from Lee's proximity and so avoid further outbursts), he left a note bequeathing the condo to Lee. He left feeling something like satisfaction, partly because guilt compelled him to make the gesture to the one who had been so kind to him, but mostly out of a desire to be free of any future obligations now that they had used part of the settlement to pay off the balance of their mortgage.

The apartment (damp and in need of painting, stinking of stale cooking smells and some faint chemical residue), recently abandoned by some disreputable character, hadn't been cleaned between tenants. In his cursory examination of the shelves and cupboards Kevin found a loaded gun that he left untouched, comforted by the presence of something so passive and yet so powerful in his meager home. Cheaply as he could he bought a bed big enough to be fucked in and whatever furniture and other household goods – the bare minimum – he needed to eat and read and live. His favorite books were piled against the walls of his bedroom. A laptop that played his pornographic DVDs sat on the kitchen table, always on, always connected to the world of men looking for a man like Kevin who was eager to take their seed, alerting Kevin to their call as he read and reread the Brontes, Dickens, Austen, Thackery, Trollope, James, Hardy, and Woolf.

He was treated for the clap, tested for syphilis, but did not stop getting fucked. He refused any other intervention, so focused was he on the only physical relief he'd found to the static colorlessness of his life. Knowing that the addition of pain would increase his relief from the stolid gray blandness, Kevin haunted the leather bars and their back rooms dressed as he had seen his pornographic role models dressed, in chaps, harness and vest. Now men beat his ass with a gloved hand or belt, twisted his nipples, held him by the throat long enough to instill, in his faint appreciation of such things, the hope for annihilation. He was never so close to feeling happy as when he returned to his dingy apartment just before dawn, bruised and aching, his ass dripping blood and cum. On these mornings, in those few seconds before drifting off to sleep, he felt content, even at peace.

It was, of course, only a matter of time before Lee found him, either by plan or by chance. Those who knew them saw Kevin in his new haunts, places where Lee would otherwise never go, and word eventually reached Lee of where Kevin could be found – and of what he was doing there. Lee's appearance at the Eagle that night was like the Bad Fairy's visitation at Sleeping Beauty's Christening: Noisy, distressing and very unwelcome. He grabbed Kevin by the locked chain around his throat, swore at him, cursed him, spat in his face, and finally struck him hard enough to knock Kevin against the wall with such force that the impact echoed through the bar, causing a momentary pause in the otherwise constant buzz of conversation. No one intervened, of course, Kevin's reputation being such that bystanders assumed it was all part of a planned and negotiated scene: the deep, demented psychodrama of formerly reputable homosexuals who had recently eschewed *bourgeois* respectability. But when Kevin was slammed against the wall with that loud and distressing thud, it was his head that hit it first. Then something extraordinary happened.

Yes, I am a notorious romantic and will, as usual, provide you, The Common Reader with a happy ending. But please remember that this is fiction. In doing my research for this romance of erotic possibilities, I learned that while much is known about the brain and how it functions after an injury, there is still more that is not understood. Think of this story, then, as a black and white movie made Before the War, one wherein the writer projects his deepest desire into an otherwise disturbing tale. Experts might roll their eyes at the coming conclusion, but even they are compelled to admit that not enough is known to absolutely refute my fable of love challenged. And even if they can refute it, why should they want to when suspended disbelief is so essential to the enjoyment of any erotica?

Kevin wept. Everything unfelt for the past year suddenly gushed forward with tears, sobs and broken sentences: a confusion of joy and pain, of angst and pleasure, that fell into a single proverbial pile at the core of his being, a muddled mess of emotions, all fragments with jagged edges. Knowing that Kevin was constitutionally unable to fake tears, Lee gathered his husband in his arms, held him close, and took him outside into the cool autumn air. Eventually Lee loaded him into their car, secured him in his seat, and took him back to their condo with the downtown view. By the time they were in the elevator, Kevin was better able to stifle his sobs, but this meager control was lost when he saw the dog's excitement on seeing the return of his long lost friend.

They went straight to bed. Lee held Kevin all night, even after the sobs subsided. Eventually they slept, the dog snoring quietly at their feet.

When they awoke it was not like it was before the accident. It never could or would be the same again. Something had returned, however, some vital fragment fallen back into place, and they awoke making love for the first time in over a year. Kevin was eager to please

Lee in anyway he could, remembering again the inner map of Lee's flesh and the secret soft places that made Lee writhe under Kevin's touch.

May I not do what I wish with my characters – even if their actions horrify The Common Reader? I know the inner workings of these men better than you do, and I am compelled to proceed to the coming finish – pun intended. I can't help it if you're yearning for some simple one-handed tale (many of which the I'm not ashamed to have written) that relies on the formula recurrent to every gay skin magazine: Ten pages with sex on the first page, an upbeat ending. No this tale must wend it's way to it's own conclusion, and to one that might be other than what The Common Reader prefers. And now I have to ask you to remember that Thanos *and* Eros *were not mere gods to the ancient Greeks but Primal Forces and, more significantly Inseparable From Birth: Where one found One, one also found the Other, like Cosmic Conjoined Twins.*

Kevin's tongue found Lee's ass hole, found the moist smoothness beckoning beyond the otherwise hairy mounds of inviting flesh. The hole, unbreached for so long, resisted his ministrations at first, and it was only with patience and persistence that the beige flower opened and gave in to the onslaught it craved. Kevin's cock, truly tumescent for the first time since the accident, glistened with pre cum and spit as it found the familiar hole, the place where it had once been so welcome. As Kevin entered Lee, they looked into each other's eyes for confirmation:

Yes, I want you and all that you are.
No, we can never be separated again.
Yes, what you have I must have too.
No, I do not want to live without you so take me with you when you die.

Kevin passed the first sphincter and gasped with pleasure. Lee sharply inhaled, so unused was he now to the girth of Kevin's (or any other) cock. Kevin watched Lee's face until he saw it relax, then pulled out an inch before moving forward another two. Lee's body tensed, but did not for a moment recoil. Sweat poured off both their bodies even though they had hardly begun to fuck, their bodies trembling with shared anticipation. Their excitement was as mutual as the coming sacrament was necessary.

Now Kevin moved with more deliberation, in then out, finding those centers of pleasure inside Lee's velvety fuckhole. Kevin watched Lee's face, the beatific grin, the angelic composure, as Kevin's rhythm doubled. Kevin could not hold off very long. He was too excited, too eager, too in love.

"Are you sure?" he gasped between strokes.

"Yes!"

"This is what you want?"

"Yes!"

"It's not too late I can still —"

But Lee grabbed Kevin's face and kissed him hard, sent his tongue down Kevin's throat. He knew the kiss would send Kevin over the edge and into oblivion. Then came the gushing of cum, the unleashing fury of so much unspent lust, of so much unspilled seed. Kevin's breaths came in short gasps. His body convulsed. He collapsed into his beloved's arms and continued their kiss. When their mouths finally released each other, they looked again into each other's eyes. There would be no going back now. The sacrament was almost complete.

Lee rolled Kevin over onto the bed, onto the sweat soaked spot he had just occupied. He turned Kevin over onto his stomach and shoved his cock inside him without so much as spit. His cock was bigger than Kevin's so it hurt all the more. The assault drew blood, but both knew that it must, that Lee must have his due now, that Kevin must be punished. Lee pounded into Kevin, cursing him the whole while, uttering words he'd never have spoken before to one he loved beyond words:

"Fucking bitch whore!"

"Yes!"

"Son of a bitch bastard slut!"

"Yes!"

"Fucking skank cum bucket!"

"Yes!"

Lee smacked Kevin's ass hard with his open hands, again, and again, until he felt his palms sting.

"Cock sucking faggot!"

"Yes!"

"Fucking cesspool!"

"Yes!"

Lee held off longer than Kevin had been able to. He wanted to prolong the punishment to add to the injury he was inflicting on the one he so desperately needed. He laid right on top of Kevin, wrapping an arm around Kevin's throat, tightening the grip as he came closer to cumming, choking Kevin when he came in great gushes, not knowing for sure (but suspecting, even hoping) that Kevin blacked out as Lee spilled so much seed deep inside him.

Later that day they went to the dingy little apartment off of Halsted Street to collect Kevin's books, clothes and laptop. Kevin remembered the gun (still loaded, still untouched), and checking with a quick glance that it was still there, was glad to firmly shut the door on it and the comfort it had once threatened.

Lee and Kevin stayed together, but things were never the same for they were no longer the same men. Their shared intellectual life returned to it's former richness as long as it was limited to books, plays and films that Kevin was familiar with before the accident – fortunately this provided a nearly inexhaustible resource.

Kevin still floundered at times, unable to find the right words, confused at the depth of others' emotions, unsure of what task next needed doing. He felt his emotions profoundly now, but with the same depth and certainty as the dog felt his, uncomplicated by contradicting passions or subtle colorations. Often confused, and always rudderless, he followed the orders Lee left for him each morning lest Kevin slip back into the habit of spending his days cruising on line:

Vacuum and dust after you walk the dog.

Then scrub the bathroom until it sparkles. Go to the gym and remember to eat lunch. Play outside with the dog in the afternoon. Bring in the mail. Make dinner. Be prepared for punishment.

Kevin obeyed, and like the dog, was happiest in obedience. He accepted punishment with pleasure for he knew from whence it came, and how much he needed Lee to feel whole. They rarely spoke of their new arrangement, only accepted it and the joy it brought them. They did not clothe it in leather and perform for the common crowd, nor did they name it. It simply was, and that was enough for both of them.

Lee was once more content, albeit in a different way than he had been before the accident. He felt his hands were full with two dogs now instead of just one – even if one of them read and walked on two feet. He loved Kevin with a firm hand as much as with a hard cock and willing hole. They made love as often as they had before, though how they made it had changed remarkably, and Kevin anticipated his punishments as eagerly as the dog did his walks. When friends or family saw the new depth of Kevin's devotion to Lee (so dog-like that it made many uncomfortable), they asked how the two were getting on, expecting some innocuous answer. Lee was always the one to respond:

"We've reached an acceptable level of dysfunction."

Everyone sensed it was better not to ask for more details than that.

BUTCH BOTTOM AND AN ABSENT DADDY

If men could live all their lives as virtuously and introspectively as when they're in love, we'd all be gods, and there'd be no need of promises of heaven or of hell.

– John Horne Burns

1. Butch Bottom

A year before Craig died, he and Jon had moved to Seattle, a place where it was easier to be over forty than San Francisco had been, where they already had some friends, where they both found jobs, and where more condo could be bought for the same money. Then Craig died so suddenly that Jon's initial response to the announcement was, "But his CD4 count has been great since he's been on the cocktail!" Forgetting, as all his friends had forgotten, that one could die of things other than the plague that had haunted them for twenty years, he was dumbfounded.

To have beaten the odds for so long and then to die of heart disease: The irony did not escape Jon, but neither was it appreciated.

Jon's life was, now that he was well into his forties, relatively placid. He lived almost alone in a large condo on First Hill with a view of the Puget Sound, the kind of view they never could have afforded in San Francisco. He had also found the proverbial dream job that paid him well for the benefit of his experience. That he should get paid more money for less of his time amused him, and would have made Craig laugh, he often thought. And Ben, too, for that matter.

"Why do you stay in such a large place if it's just you?" someone had asked.

"I have a lot of ghosts," Jon wanted to say.

Instead he just shrugged his shoulders and mumbled something about resale value. But the ghosts were there: Ben, his first Sir; Craig, his second; the two muttly dogs that had been Ben's and then his and Craig's; countless friends. Sometimes he wandered from room to room, most of them half empty, looking at his Museum of the Dead: Photographs on the walls, paintings and books left to him in wills, odd pieces of furniture from the estates of friends, souvenirs of his lives (for there had been two very distinct lives) in Los Angeles and then San Francisco, boxes of theatre programs, magazines, and mementos from marches and rallies, dance parties and festivals: Relics from a lost world.

Over all of it presided a magnificent mackerel Maine Coon named Schrödinger. He sat on high in whatever room Jon happened to be in, presiding over his dominion, guarding Jon from his ghosts, licking away the silent tears when they came. Content to be alone all day with a warm place to sleep and the radio left on NPR, somewhere to watch the rain and a table lamp to sit under, each evening Schrödinger greeted Jon quietly with a raised head and soft meow before stretching awake and asking to be picked up.

"How was your day, Schro?" Jon would ask, as he used to ask Ben's dogs. Having not been raised with animals, he hadn't understood their mysteries or their importance before living with Ben. Now he understood the comfort and company they offered. Now he appreciated, more than ever, the pleasure of not being alone in an empty apartment or, worse, an empty bed.

Jon was a Top as much out of necessity as out of desire. He had always been a switch in the field but a bottom at home, having found not one but two Sirs to love him in turn. But being alone and over forty, meant being a Top – at least if he wanted to get laid, for, as always, boys were plentiful and Daddies fewer. Boys came and went, boys of all ages, all of them poz: Boys he could flog and fuck, boys he could beat and breed. A few tried to reach out to touch Jon's heart only to find it shielded, unreachable behind an armor made from loss and regret. Jon appreciated the effort but knew it unfair to let them pursue their course. These boys he stopped welcoming to his playroom, sending them away as much out of kindness as out of self-preservation: For he was never satisfied unless there were tears in a boy's eyes. To demand this of someone who wanted love would have been nothing short of cruel – and cruel in a bad way, he was quick to add while explaining his dilemma to his friends over beers and ciders at Six Arms.

"I've only just learned to take care of myself again," he told his friends. "I'm not going to start taking care of someone else, too."

His friends refrained from pointing out the obvious, that Jon was already taking care of a cat as devoted to him as he was to the cat, that his heart had never stopped beating but only retreated in order to heal. Why else would he spend so much time listening to music about love, '50s and '60s jazz, upbeat and sad, bitter and sweet: Music that ran the gamut of love lest any nuance be misremembered or forgotten. This was a heart, Jon's friends well knew, preparing to love again.

Typical of the boys he fucked was Danny. Scruffy and sweet, a shy smile and flawless body, a beautiful mouth perfect for both kissing and fucking, and big brown eyes that glistened with tears when the pain became unbearable, winning Jon's attention as few had since Craig's death. Nothing was sweet as a salty kiss, as tear stained lips, as grateful surrender. Nothing got his cock so hard. The teary kiss was followed by a fast, furious and brutal fuck that left Danny sobbing with gratitude, often climaxing without touching himself – his hands bound behind him the whole time – and as spent as Jon. But Danny, for all his charms, wanted nothing more from Jon than this. Jon was one of many men he surrendered to on a frequent basis, each man knowing that the man who would some day own Danny had yet to enter his life. But he warmed Jon's heart with his sobs and tears, his agony comforting Jon time after time, giving him a peaceful night's sleep.

Jon was on a date with a man he'd met on line, someone close to his age who claimed to be both "versatile and masculine, UB2." Like most men who insist on their masculinity, the need to do so sprang from the world's apparent blindness to the exact degree of his machismo. Jon was ambivalent as the rest of the world within ten minutes of their meeting face to face, but not wanting to be rude, suggested the man accompany him to Chop Suey to see a new queer band he'd heard about from Danny.

They arrived just as the band was starting, the handsome lead singer (bearded and golden, green eyed and amber) singing a song Jon had never heard before, a song about some stranger's Pretty Mouth. The rest of the crowd was younger than Jon and his date, but Jon found himself nodding to the boys in the crowd he already knew sexually and otherwise. He handed his date a drink just as the band started **Stony End**.

"I can't believe he's singing a Streisand song. Is this supposed to be ironic?"

"Streisand wasn't the first one to record the song, and, no, it's not irony."

"Isn't it about getting knocked-up?"

"It was, but not when he sings it."

"I'm sure you're wrong."

"I know I'm right."

Jon stepped forward, and away from his date, to better hear the lead singer explain how he got knocked-up, but knocked-up as he heard the boys in the gym use the phrase: "Did you hear about Lance? Dude, the condom broke and he got knocked-up. Sucks to be him." Jon knew at once that the singer was poz, and that he sang about his sero-conversion and the accompanying fear, and Jon understood the familiar lyrics as he had never understood them before. Then the singer segued into **Wedding Bell Blues**.

"Why the fuck is he doing this old number?"

"Don't you get it? It's a protest song when he sings it. This is where the irony comes in."

"I'm bored," said his date.

"Well, please don't let me keep you. I think these guys are great and I want to hear them."

Jon gave his date the perfunctory kiss goodbye and moved closer to the stage to better see the singer. Jon was entranced with the band, with the singer's beauty, with the lyrics to their original songs, to the choice of old songs interpreted in new ways. The singer's masculinity was unquestioned as he sang about sex with men, about heartbreak and desire.

"Great, huh?"

Jon turned and saw the familiar face of Danny, shirtless with the top button of his 501s undone as they rode down his hips.

"Hey, baby."

Jon gave Danny a kiss and let his hand migrate down Danny's spine to his ass.

"And he's famous for wearing fewer and fewer clothes as the night progresses. See, he just took of his shirt."

Jon looked at the muscular body covered with fine silky hair and slick with sweat. Another song started, slow and familiar.

"Oh, this is so cool, Dad. This is when the straight boys dance together."

Danny pulled Jon to one side and, true to Danny's word, the straight boys left their dates and paired up, some dancing cheek to cheek, others nuzzling each other affectionately. One pair, as if on a dare, even kissed. Jon recognized the old show tune, now being sung as a rock ballad, as "You're My Romance" albeit with a B inserted before the last word. The song ended and the crowd cheered. The boys, some of them still arm in arm, went back to their dates. The girls, excited by the sight of two men together, threw themselves at their boyfriends, partly to reclaim them, and partly to reward them for the public foreplay.

Jon's hand slipped inside the back of Danny's jeans and fingered the moist hole.

"You're already wet."

"Afraid so. Turn you on?"

"Fuck, yeah."

They kissed, embraced, and sucked face for several minutes before Jon guided Danny out of the club, his hand on Danny's ass the whole time. They were unaware of the sad envy in the singer's brilliant green eyes as he began singing **He's a Rebel** – *sans* irony.

A few nights later, Jon and several of his friends congregated at Purr. Ordering drinks, it was several minutes before Jon saw Leo approach the tiny karaoke stage after being introduced by one of the staff. It was few more minutes before Jon recognized him.

"Hey isn't he the singer from that band, the…"

"Butch Bottom and the Absent Daddies?"

"Yeah. Isn't that him?"

"Must be, no two men could be that handsome in the same way."

Jon leaned forward, his face with its salt and pepper beard framed in the reflected light from the stage. Hearing Leo croon **It Had to Be You**. Jon forgot his drink, let the ice melt in the glass and dilute the liquor as he nodded with the music.

"What's his name again?" Jon asked the cocktail waitress bringing a refill he wouldn't touch.

"Leo Lourea. Cute, huh?"

Jon nodded.

Reluctantly, Jon left with his friends just as Leo's song ended. When he got home, he held Schrödinger close, wondering what had just happened to him. A few days later, as if the gods conspired with more coordination than customary, he found out:

They reached the door of the Eagle at the same moment. There was a nod, a short greeting, and some mutual admiration as Jon assessed Leo's interest. Face to face, it was easy to see that they were about the same height with similar builds, though Jon had the weight of maturity, the grizzled beard and chest hair that said "Daddy". Still, each man having friends to meet and greet at the bar, it was a almost half an hour before they ran into each other again, drifting to that dark corner by the pool table found in every bar called The Eagle. There was another nod and their mouths met without hesitation; their hands grappled beneath each other's gear to grab the glory of the other's manhood. They kissed and groped for an hour or more, unable to free their selves from the embrace, not wanting to escape except into each other.

"We'll go to my place," muttered Jon between kisses.

"Yes, Sir," was all Leo managed to say before dropping to his knees nuzzling Jon's crotch.

"Good boy."

"By the way," whispered Leo between kisses. "I'm poz."

"I figured. Me too."

They left hand in hand, kissing occasionally until they turned up Terry Street.

"No fucking way, Dad. You live here too?"

And now they laughed to discover that they had lived in the same building for more than a year but had never met until now, the gods guarding Jon from seeing the one he would love before he was ready.

Kisses continued in the elevator. When the door opened and they moved into Jon's too large apartment, their endeavors to undress each other became frantic, their breath caught in quick gasps. Jon tried to move Leo towards the bedroom, but they never made it there. Soon Jon's face was buried in Leo's ass, then Leo's face buried in Jon's pubic hair. There were cries for relief from the anguish of tumescence, tiny howls from deep within, primal grunts and growls they were unaware of making until Leo grabbed Jon's thick cock and eased it towards his hole and whispered.

"Please, Sir, no jacket. Just fuck me, Dad."

Jon complied with just spit for lube, felt the sudden joy of penetrating the perfect tawny ass, a luscious pink hole sprayed with the light dusting of red-gold fur. He held Leo down as he fucked him, slapped his ass, a stream of explicatives coursing from an otherwise gentle voice. He rammed into Leo as hard as he could, eager to have him, eager to embrace the profound beauty squirming beneath him, eager to leave his mark of ownership. He came with a scream, with the primal call of man taking man, of a man making another man his own, the ancient cry of the conqueror that echoed back so many millennia. He collapsed on top of Leo to recover his presence of mind. He reached underneath Leo to see if he was hard only to discover that while this was indeed true, Leo had also cum. Jon rolled off of his sudden conquest, pleased with himself and the one who had so quickly become the vessel of his seed.

"So," asked Leo, breathless between each word, "what's your name, Dad?"

As if on cue, Schrödinger walked into the room with an almost human cry to announce his presence. He greeted Jon with a lick on the nose before introducing himself to Leo and accepting the newcomer's homage. When satisfied, he took his place on a nearby ottoman, watching them through half-closed eyes.

"Excellent cat."

"Yes," agreed Jon, happy to be relieved of the burden of self-disclosure by the cat's presence. "I inherited him." And from those three words came the story of his life, elicited from the inevitable question:

"Who from, Sir?"

It came like a torrent, the tale of life with Ben followed by widowhood in Los Angeles, meeting Craig and moving to San Francisco for twelve happy years grabbed from the Fates that ended after their move to Seattle only a few months before the same Fates, as if making the cruelest of jests, struck Craig down with a heart attack. Leo heard all this with an open heart, leaned over Jon's handsome, bearded face and kissed him with more tenderness than Jon had known in years, bringing him as much pain as comfort as the shell protecting his heart shattered like an eggshell. A few minutes later they were showering together, continually kissing as if for nourishment.

For the first time in more than two years, Jon dared to hope.

"This is ridiculous," Jon told a friend the next day. "He's barely thirty, and I'm... a lot older than him."

"But how does he make you feel?"

"Alive," confessed Jon for the first time. "And happy."

Their courtship proceeded without pause. They saw each other everyday, if only for a meal. They made love, fucked, and played constantly. And kissed, desperately. Jon went to hear Leo perform either alone or with the Absent Daddies. Leo took to dedicating songs to "my sweet Daddy," making Jon blush with pride and embarrassment. When Leo crooned love songs alone at Purr, he looked right at Jon as he sang, his voice taking on a timber, a new authority that, for all his experiences with men before Jon, it had lacked until now.

That they were both desperately happy was evident. Schrödinger now expected Leo as well as Jon, apparently pleased that order had been restored with the presence of two men in his bed instead of the mere one.

"You can't argue with a cat," Craig had said when Schrödinger had selected him at the animal shelter years before. Remembering this, Jon turned to the cat for guidance.

"Is this really what I need, Schro? Is this what I want?"

Cats, however, tend to be inscrutable when presented with a direct question and Jon had to observe Schrödinger's behavior for an answer.

One morning in late summer, Jon found himself alone in bed. He got up to pee wondering if Leo had already left for his day job. He opened the bedroom door and saw Leo, naked and facing the early morning sun as it flashed off the skyscrapers of downtown Seattle. He was rocking back and forth, softly singing, as if in prayer. Jon cocked an ear and listened carefully. He recognized the Hebrew hymn, for it had been sung at both of the funerals that had marred his happiness. When Leo was finished singing, sobs, soft manly cries of honest pain and loss, emerged from the trembling, naked figure.

Jon came up behind Leo, wrapped his arms around Leo, and kissed the back of his head, his shoulders.

"Baby," he whispered. "Sweet, sweet baby boy. What's wrong?"

"I woke up and remembered that this is the day Uncle Ori died."

Leo turned around in his lover's arms, facing Jon with tear stained eyes.

"He died when I was fifteen. He and Uncle Cary used to look after me all the time. And then they both died."

"Baby, I'm so sorry. I didn't know. Should we visit their graves today?"

Leo nodded the affirmative, almost smiling.

Jon kissed away Leo's tears, tasting their salty sweetness with a new kind of appreciation as Schrödinger wended his way between and around their legs, making small cries asking for inclusion in their affection, or maybe for breakfast, but probably both.

"And now?" ask Jon's friends when he told them this story.

"Now do you believe this is right?"

"We all think so."

"In fact, if you break up, we all plan on keeping him as a friend."

"We're all crazy about him."

"The question is, are you?"

Leo demonstrated his devotion in so many ways, ways that said, "You're the Daddy I've always wanted. Be my Sir, and I will love you for the rest of my life." He cooked for Jon, looked after him, gave him space to spend time with friends, never asked him where he'd been on the rare occasions Jon hadn't been there to hear him sing, was always willing to be used by either Jon or any man Jon chose, and only asked for the occasional beating. He never spoke of love to Jon, only murmured the words to Schrödinger, just to make his intentions known.

Everyone waited, Jon, Leo, and all their friends, for the dam to break. They waited as summer turned to fall, as the rains returned to the Puget Sound, and a wet frigidity settled over a city covered in fallen leaves.

Snow fell, and as was the habit with this city, most people stayed home from work. Only the essential commuted into or out of the city. Even though Jon walked to work, he knew there was no urgent need to get there since nearly everyone else would stay home. He would work from home today, taking care of anything urgent but leaving the mundane until tomorrow.

Snuggled beneath the down comforter, Jon felt Leo's arms wrap around him. He moved closer to Leo only to feel Leo's fat cock searching for Jon's fuckhole, an orifice nearly forgotten for a year or more. Leo moved closer, the slick head finding and poking the hole, softly piercing the hairy maw. Jon cried out in pain but didn't resist. He let Leo take the lead, let him find the secret soft place deep inside him, the hard knot that would make him cry out in pleasure. It hurt. Jon bit the pillow, submitted to Leo's assault, silently begged for more because the brilliant fire now searing through him touched his heart, burning away that final residue (like the membrane of egg beneath it's shell) and sent Jon into the sweet oblivion of pleasure and pain.

"Sweet ass, Dad"

"Fuck me."

"You want your boy's cum inside you? You want to be your boy's bitch?"

"Fucking breed me."

Leo obeyed. He forced his way deep inside Jon.

Jon could feel a small trickle of blood trailing down his balls but didn't ask Leo to stop. Instead he pushed back when Leo pulled out. Leo bit the back of Jon's neck, held Jon down as Jon had held him down so many times. The bed covers fell to the floor. Leo slapped Jon's ass just to feel Jon's hole quiver around his cock, just to get closer to his goal. He'd cum the night before while getting fucked by Jon, but he was young and a morning hard-on demanded attention.

"Bitch Daddy!"

"Fuck me, fuck me…"

"I'm gonna cum, Daddy. You want your boy's cum inside you?"

"Yes, yes, please."

Leo cried out his final pleasure, the momentary eternity, as he marked the man he loved with the liquor of his manhood. A moment passed and they were back in bed together, both coming to as if from a blackout. Then Jon realized that he was weeping. For one desperate moment, he thought he'd been unmanned, made less of the Dad he wanted to be for Leo. But Leo rolled him over and kissed him. His silent tears, they both knew, were tears of joy. There was a pool of jizz on the sheet where Jon had cum while Leo fucked him. It was not until then that Jon realized that he'd climaxed, that he had let himself feel pleasure and pain as he had not let himself feel anything since Craig had died. It was true then, and Jon had no choice but to tell Leo that truth:

"I love you, baby boy. Please stay with me, baby. Stay with me forever."

So many seconds passed before Leo answered, each second a beat of his heart, each an eternity.

"Oh, Daddy, Sir, of course I'll stay with you. I love you so much. I love you so much it hurts."

And as they kissed again, their kiss the seal on the bargain that would be their future together, Jon wondered: Which is saltier, tears or cum? And which the sweeter?

2. An Absent Daddy

Leo was fortunate not only to be born at a time when ethnic ambiguity was fashionable, but in a city where it was almost inevitable. Descended from African nobility sold into slavery, Swedish peasant farmers raised to the status of gentry, Snohomish elders that lead their nation, and once wealthy Sephardim with bloodlines so ancient they might laugh at American *poseurs* like the First Families of Virginia, Leo was strikingly handsome with features that suggested rather than demonstrated his ancestry. As a result, his lovers (and there were many) saw in him what they wanted to see, and embraced that part of the world they most desired. He was as tawny as his name's sake, with bold features and high cheekbones complimented by a dusting of freckles, wavy auburn hair and a luxurious beard, his hard, muscular body covered with red-blond hair. Able to blush, his golden skin was set off by the delectable pink of his lips, nipples, butt hole and cock head. Best of all, he had no idea how beautiful he was.

When he was eight years old, Leo took to singing "It's Raining Men" as he danced around the house. His parents, left-wing intellectuals, assumed the obvious and arranged that Leo should spend more time with Uncle Ori and Uncle Cary (who were already in the habit of spoiling Leo and his older siblings) so that Leo might grow up with the expectation of finding love. Leo's favorite memories were of falling asleep on their couch, snuggled between his uncles, as they watched **The Wizard of Oz**, **Auntie Mame**, **Mary Poppins**, or **Gentlemen Prefer Blondes**. In the morning he'd wake up in "his" room with Sheba, his Uncles' dog, stretched out at the foot of his bed guarding him (so Uncle Cary insisted) from any nightmares.

When the Uncles died within six months of each other just before Leo turned 16, he was almost inconsolable, finding solace only in the music and movies they had shared with him. His entire family, equally bereft, pulled on their multiple traditions, providing the many kinds of spiritual comfort that Leo came to rely on later in life. He learned to pray to Whomever it seemed most appropriate, repeating prayers in languages he might not know, finding in the rhythm of the syllables the solace of a mantra. And as a result of his parents' insight Leo never Came Out with a declarative statement, but rather with the introduction of his first boyfriend, Seth, less than a year later. That Seth was so fearful of sex and infection that he confined their physical expressions of affection to dry kissing and mutual masturbation might have been a relief to Leo's parents (had they known) but it was frustrating to Leo who knew (if only from finding his Uncles' stash of pornography) that sex might be so much more.

After Leo's break-up with Seth (just after their prom), he sought more of what had looked so appealing on video. Now in his majority, he was able to pursue the adult men he actively desired. Soon he was experimenting with men he met online or at the baths. Willing and able to try just about anything, he found he enjoyed most of it, taking and giving whatever pleasures were presented to him. There was no love at first, or the need for it, only affection and respect – and for a while, that was enough. His boyfriends came and went, rarely becoming anything too serious, for when they did Leo felt forced to abandon them to their own devices. He was neither needing nor prepared for True Love as long as there were more men ready to do him than he had time for each weekend. He loved the Circuit and had more fun than he was able to remember after each party in Palm Springs, South Beach, San Francisco, New York or Chicago. Although conscious of being something of a star, Leo also knew that he didn't want to be on the Circuit too long. He feared becoming one of those fossils desperately dancing in a drugged daze pretending to be something he no longer was. Someday it would be time to retire and build a nest. With each birthday, the itch to settle down, to be done with the Circuit, increased. Each weekend party, he promised himself, would the last. And then, after one particularly profligate weekend in Palm Springs, Leo realized that he had at last gone to far and that it was time to find The Man Who Would Take Him Home, a man, whom Leo now knew, would have to be poz.

Thus, his sero-conversion was the impetus for many changes in his life, including abandoning the Circuit while he was still young enough to be missed. He blamed no one but himself – for no one had forced him to swallow the X that weekend just as no one had forced him to bend over and take all and sundry uncovered cocks up his cleaned and prelubed ass. After the bad news (hardly unexpected), the Circuit lost its glamour and Leo focused on finding the kind of life his Uncles had shared. Now it was time to nest; now he was the same age as his older siblings had been when they married.

First he focused on his band, Butch Bottom and the Absent Daddies, which gave him the voice he wanted to share with the world. They became well known for singing original songs like **Bad Touch**, **Show Me on the Doll**, and **Jack Daniels Tastes Like Daddy's Kisses** as well as standards like **Jailhouse Rock**, **I Sold My Heart to the Junkman**, and **Love Potion Number Nine** that took on new meanings when performed by the Absent Daddies. On other nights, he sang karaoke in cocktail lounges like Purr, crooning the same ballads his Uncles had danced to around their living room.

His day job, laying tile in the posher homes of the Puget Sound, was an art he'd learned from his much loved paternal grandfather. Having done it most of his life, Leo didn't think much about the gift passed down to him through the generations; instead, he just enjoyed his work, singing to himself all the while, finding the perfect phrasing, the right cadence, the proper *cris de coeur* to make each song his own. The demand for his talent as a mosaic artist (for that was what he was) allowed him to make his own hours, and his clients granted him all the privileges due creative talent.

Shortly before his thirtieth birthday, Leo moved to a small but stylish condo on First Hill. From his bedroom he could see the Space Needle piercing the heavens – the same heavens his Snohomish grandmother had once told him were raised high above the trees only when the native nations surrounding the Puget Sound came together and pushed the sky up high above the trees with their combined strength. On his first New Year's Eve in the condo, he invited friends to watch the fireworks ejaculating from the Space Needle at midnight before they headed to the Eagle.

His bedroom was now his nest high above the world, the private domain he hoped to share with the man he'd yet to meet.

One night at Chop Suey, when the band still had third billing below Loss of Function, Purty Mouth, and Tractor Sex Fatality, two straight girls came up to the stage between songs.

"Hey like we made our boyfriends promise to dance together so could you guys do like a slow song?"

"Only if you make them kiss, too."

"Ohmigod that is so awesome yeah!"

"Totally awesome they gotta do it even if it means we have to blow 'em later."

"Totally!"

Assured that a kiss would be part of the deal, the band played **My Buddy**, a song they often did as a rock ballad, slowing it down a notch for the occasion. Sure enough, the boys danced together, cheek to cheek. When the song ended, they kissed each other perfunctorily on the lips, mouths closed, to the delighted squeals of their girlfriends. From this grew a tradition for the band, one that not only assured its increasing popularity among a generation of young adults who found the display of boy-on-boy dancing not only titillating, but proof of machismo for the young men dancing. From then on, when the band sang **My Buddy**, the straight boys danced together, some looking desperately for a partner when the song was announced for fear of being thought less of a man for being unwilling to participate. So popular did the song become, the band added **You're My Bromance**, a pun that delighted the young men as much as their dates. Sometimes single straight men even brought their gay buddies so they could be seen dancing together and so solicit the attention of the young women they wanted to meet.

Leo would always remember the time he first saw Jon. He was at Six Arms, sitting with the Absent Daddies after a gig, when Jon walked past him, joking with his buddies about the wet wind lashing the windows of the pub and saying that real men didn't need umbrellas. Leo had never seen a man more desirable than Jon, salt and pepper hair and beard, and (despite the inevitable tummy) the naturally hard, muscular body of man who had been pumping iron for decades without the benefit of chemical additives. Leo watched him leave as his friends teased him.

"Leo likes his Daddy Bears."

"Huh?"

"Wipe the drool off your beard, Leo. He's gone now."

Leo forced a weak smile.

"A man's dick has a mind of it's own, you know."

Only a few nights, later, singing his song for the straight boys, Leo saw Jon the audience talking to a young man Leo knew only in passing. When Jon left with the other boy, Leo thought his heart might break. It was only when he saw Jon again at Purr a few nights later that Leo thought the gods might be on side after all. Jon's face was blissful in the reflected light, eyes half-closed as he nodded to the music. Leo sang to Jon, wondering if Jon knew what was happening between them, that Leo had made love to him with words and music, with a heart that needed a home.

It seemed an eternity to Leo, but it was less then two weeks between the first encounter and the moment Leo found himself bent over Jon's leather couch. When Jon ejaculated inside him, Leo squeezed hard with all his interior muscle to milk every last drop of jism, to keep it all deep inside him for as long as possible so that he might feel owned by Jon. He had no idea, just yet, that Jon was just as enamored of him. It was only when Jon spilled the story of his life, so quickly and with so little time to breathe for fear of sobbing before this suddenly intimate stranger that Leo understood how vulnerable Jon was. In that vulnerability Leo found the foothold that would lead to the capture of Jon's heart. He relied on every love song he'd ever sung to win Jon, on every kiss, and on each cry of pain he could convince Jon to illicit from him.

Their courtship began with an immediate invitation to dinner followed by Leo making their breakfast the next morning. It felt natural to Jon for Leo to be rattling the pots and pans in his kitchen, too normal for comfort even, and Leo sensed Jon's simultaneous appreciation and dismay. Leo, with the inner wisdom of the Lover, said nothing and made no demands. He left Jon's side the next morning knowing that Jon would call him, that his absence would feel as wrong as his companionship felt right. Just to be sure, though, he held Schrödinger a moment before he left, asking the cat's permission to love the man they had slept with the night before. The cat, pleased with Leo's manners, assented, and Leo left it to the cat to work the needed *mojo*.

Before the day was over, Jon called Leo's mobile phone and Leo asked him to meet him at Purr. Jon came and sat as close to the karaoke stage as he dared, drinking little except Leo's voice, his song a spell that wove itself around Jon like a net, forcing him to breathe the air that he had for so long avoided, and so find himself renewed. After singing, they sat in a corner of the club kissing, touching, each unsure of the other's tangibility. Leo had become a vessel with their first kiss, a cavity that longed to be filled with Jon's kisses, cock, cum, and affection. Now he let his kisses speak for him, as his song had done before. He had not known how much he wanted to live his life with a man until he met the man he wanted to live with, until he understood how deep desire can run in a man's soul.

"You love him," said the drummer, the only female Absent Daddy, an athletic baby dyke frequently mistaken for a boy.

"I think so," admitted Leo, afraid to say anything more definite.

"Yeah, you are. And he's a babe, too."

"You think so, too?"

"Oh, yeah. What are you waiting for?"

"For him. He's been widowed twice."

"Broken hearts heal," said the drummer reaching across the table and taking Leo's hand. "You just have to give him time. I see how he looks at you. He wants you bad, real bad, and I'm not just talking about that sweet butt of yours."

Leo blushed, started to disagree but didn't. He'd seen the same look in Jon's eyes. Each time he saw it, his heart danced in his chest and he felt short of breath, hoping desperately that Jon would say the words Leo wanted to hear. Then Jon would look quickly away, suddenly fearful as he been hopeful a moment earlier, and Leo knew that he had to wait until pain gave birth to joy – or until Jon started making excuses for not seeing him. One or the other would have to happen.

Even on that summer morning when Leo woke up and knew without looking at the calendar that it was his uncle's *yartzheit*, even when Jon had been so sweet and understanding, even after all those months, Leo waited. He didn't dare push, didn't dare ask Jon how he felt. When Jon made plans without him, he told Leo ahead of time but hurried home to call Leo as soon as he could. Leo made a point of going out without Jon. Sometimes he played *Mah Jong* with the men he met through Jon, spending an afternoon or an evening away from Jon but well within his field of vision. Jon's friends, most of them now regular members of Leo's audience, gently prodded him, asking for more information than Leo had to give.

"You're still an item?" asked one of the men at the table.

"I hope so."

"Will there be a wedding?"

"We'll see. Mom and Dad said they'd host one if I wanted it."

"Have they met Jon?" asked a second man.

"Yes, he came for Passover. They loved him. He's a lot like them."

The friends nodded.

"And he'll come for Thanksgiving."

"And Hanukah?" asked the third.

"And Christmas and Kwanzaa."

"Is there anything you family doesn't celebrate?"

Leo thought for a moment before answering, playing his tile with cool deliberation.

"Sure there is: The Feast of the Immaculate Conception."

The snow came early that year, a few inches piled here and there across the Puget Sound's many microclimates. First Hill was without snow at first, not accumulating any on the streets until most of the surrounding neighborhoods had succumbed to it. Leo and Jon made love by Jon's fire as the snow fell outside. They made love and Leo felt closer then ever to Jon. Jon was alternately gentle and cruel, hurting Leo as much with a caress as with a blow. An open palm might lead to orgasm, a kiss to unspeakable agony. It was only when it was over that Leo realized that Jon had never been the receiver in their erotic exercises. He had cum countless times in, or on, Leo, but never had Leo been allowed to do more than suck Jon's ample cock, and even then Jon held the back of Leo's head and took control. Leo's ministrations to Jon had been limited because Jon no longer allowed himself the luxury of abandon.

Schrödinger approached them with a small meow, simultaneously disclaiming on the icy debris falling from the sky and suggesting that they all head to the bed.

"He knows when you're coming, you know."

"Really?"

"Oh, yeah. He runs to the door before you're even out of the elevator. That's how I knew you were a keeper. You can't argue with a cat."

As they kissed, Leo felt the cat's paw press on his back as if urging him to take the needed step. When they were all in Jon's bed again, safe beneath the covers, Schrödinger curled between, his face looking towards Leo. Stroking the cat, Leo felt a small nip. He looked at the cat and saw his green eyes almost glow as he slowly closed them before falling asleep. Leo understood the cat's assessment of the situation. The cat wanted them both for his companions, for having two men in his bed was the norm. Leo knew what had to be done.

Leo woke first the next morning. Looking around he saw Jon sleeping peacefully and Schrödinger sitting in the doorway, blinking slowly in greeting. Wordlessly he got up and followed the cat into the kitchen. Feeding his friend, Leo knew better than to ask for more instruction than had already been given him. Silently, he thanked the cat and headed back to bed.

A moment later he was rubbing his hard cock against Jon's hairy ass, letting it slide between the muscular butt cheeks. Jon drowsily reached back to hold him closer. Leo smiled to himself, kissed his lover's neck, and let his fat cock find Jon's bunghole.

"I need your hole, Dad," he whispered urgently.

He heard Jon gasp in pain as he pressed forward, and paused a moment. Then afraid he might lose his nerve, Leo pushed in. He felt Jon open up, felt Jon's desire for more despite the anguish of the assault. Leo forced himself in until the entire length and girth of his manhood was incased tightly in Jon's flesh. Now Leo moved slowly, murmuring encouragements, promising to take Jon to the other side of desire:

"Sweet ass, Dad"

"Fuck me."

"You want your boy's cum inside you? You want to be your boy's bitch?"

"Fucking breed me."

Jon rolled his head back and forth, clutched at the sheets, bit the pillow. Leo knew the signs of a man on the verge, knew that Jon was very close to abandoning any hope of solitude, to breaking every promise he'd made to his grief-hardened heart.

"Bitch Daddy!"

"Fuck me, fuck me…"

"I'm gonna cum, Daddy. You want your boy's cum inside you?"

"Yes, yes, please."

Then Leo heard Jon scream his joy, felt Jon's hole clench tight as Jon ejaculated against the sheets. Then Leo came, marking Jon as Jon had marked him countless times. Now Jon would be as much his as he was Jon's. Now Jon waited, an eternity of moments for the words he wished to hear. Staying inside his lover, Leo held him close, kissing Jon's neck until their flesh disengaged of it's own accord. Jon rolled over, facing Jon, silent tears staining his stubbled cheeks. Leo kissed the tears away, wondering what havoc he had wrought in fucking his Dad, in letting his need for love get the better of him – but then came the words:

"I love you, baby boy. Please stay with me, baby. Stay with me forever."

Leo took a breath and held it, repeating the words he'd just heard in his mind's ear over and over again before he answered.

"Oh, Daddy, Sir, I love you so much. I love you so much it hurts."

And Schrödinger watched from just outside the bedroom door, purring loudly, slowly kneading the carpet and working his *mojo*.

ABOUT THE AUTHOR
DAVID MAY

Starting out in life as a nice boy from a good family looking desperately for the wrong crowd, David May started writing as a child. After graduating from UC Santa Cruz, he moved to San Francisco where he initially gained notoriety in 1984 when his first story, **Cutting Threads**, which was published in *Drummer,* sparking both controversy and praise from readers. A regular contributor to *Drummer* until its demise, May's work has also appeared in *Honcho, Mach, Advocate Men, Unzipped, Inches, Frontiers, Lambda Book Report, Harvard Gay & Lesbian*  *Review, Cat Fancy, International Leatherman* and *Manifest Review*. David May's work, both fiction and nonfiction, can also be found in *Kosher Meat, Best of Gay Erotica 2003, Best of Gay Erotica 2007, Afterwords: Real Sex From Gay Men's Diaries, Bar Stories, Queer View Mirror, Flesh and the Word 3, The Mammoth Book of New Gay Erotica,*

Bears and many other anthologies. In 2002 he moved to Seattle where he lives with, and is owned by, his Sir and two cats.

David May is also the author of:

- Madrugada: A Cycle of Erotic Fictions

Find this book and others at your local bookstore, Amazon.com and TheNazcaPlainsCorp.com.

MADRUGADA

A CYCLE OF EROTIC FICTIONS

DAVID MAY

A
BONER
BOOK

www.ingramcontent.com/pod-product-compliance
Lightning Source LLC
Chambersburg PA
CBHW071228260626
47162CB00004B/1472